The Billionaire's Secretive Enchantress

Elizabeth Lennox

CONTENTS

ACKNOWLEDGMENTS

If it weren't for my family who provide continuous cheerleading support for my writing, this book would not be possible. My thanks to all of you. On a daily basis, you inspire me, make me laugh, and warm my heart with your smiles and love.

Prologue

Sierra stared at her sister closely, not understanding what was wrong. Something had disturbed her normally unflappable sister and it scared her. "Marissa, what's happened?"

She felt her sister shiver and a moment later, Marissa simply disappeared into the house. Sierra watched carefully, glancing at her father to see if he'd seen the escape as well. Hopefully not and Marissa could make a clean getaway. But as she surveyed the crowd of people around her father's luxurious pool, her father's suspicious eyes were following his eldest daughter closely. The look she saw in those dark, evil depths indicated that he definitely wasn't happy about his eldest daughter's disappearance.

Sierra was just about to try and get her sister's attention – to call Marissa back – but at that moment, her eyes, and her breath, were snagged by a tall, gorgeous man who stepped out onto the flagstone patio. She gasped, her body frozen in stunned fascination as the strange, attractive man looked around, his eyes seeming to take in all of the important details. Unfortunately, Sierra wasn't one of those details, but why would she be? A man as striking as he was wouldn't look twice at a young, skinny teenager who hadn't a hope of blossoming into the kind of woman who probably caught his eye. Even at eighteen, Sierra hadn't formed the curves of a woman, not even a hint of what might happen. It hadn't ever bothered her until this moment, until she'd seen this man. And had his eyes pass over her, barely even seeing her.

She wasn't a raving beauty. Her best asset, her long, brown hair, was tied behind her and braided down her back. That left her skinny, gangly arms and legs left for him to see and they weren't very interesting. She sometimes thought her eyes were pretty, but there was only so much one could do with boring, blue eyes.

1

In that same instant, her father noticed the man as well and Sierra's heart sank with disappointment. With a lurch, her father stepped around his contemptible minions hovering like gnats around the bar and moved over to the tall, dark haired stranger, greeting him effusively. Sierra wished with all her heart that this one man wasn't one of her father's pathetic, rock-slithering underlings. She was drawn to his earthy looks, handsome demeanor and bulging muscles that strained the fine cotton shirt stretched over his broad shoulders.

Sierra watched him with a sinking heart, wondering why he would even associate with her father and his ilk. The stranger certainly didn't look like the rest of the men surrounding the pool with their gaudy, thick, gold chains and their ill-fitting shirts, most of them with bellies that protruded repulsively over their belts. No, this new man appeared to be refined, dignified. He had no paunch at all. In fact, she suspected that he actually had ridges on that flat stomach of his. There was just something about the way he held himself, the way he walked, with confidence and elegance, that told her he worked out a great deal and took too much pride in his appearance to allow himself to get flabby.

In addition, there wasn't any jewelry on him at all, not even a tacky, pretentious, pinky ring. His white, tailored shirt was tucked neatly into his pressed slacks without any overlap. In fact, he looked more muscular than all of the men combined.

In a word, he was gorgeous!

But what was he doing here? Her father seemed to be excited to see him. She watched with growing disappointment as her father walked the man over to the others by the bar, all of them looking eager to welcome this new person into their midst simply because her father was introducing him to everyone. That was a sure sign that the stranger was important.

The men who hung around her father might not be the best and brightest at math or science, but they were experts at reading body language, understanding politics and sucking up to the important people. In other words, they had street smarts. They knew how to survive.

Sort of, she thought with sadness, since there had been men at her father's previous parties who were just as street savvy but had mysteriously disappeared.

Briefly, she noticed the man's dark eyes glance in her direction. Did he hesitate when he saw her? Or was it just her hopeful imagination? The moment was brief and, all too quickly, her father was leading the handsome stranger in the opposite direction. When the two disappeared into the house, heading towards her father's office, Sierra felt her heart melt because the only people who went into her father's office were underlings or business associates. Either alternative was…unfortunate.

She felt her body deflate as if it were a balloon, disappointed at the reality that the one man she'd met who looked fascinating, who instantly made her heart race with excitement simply because he was close by, was nothing more than a minion or yet another petty criminal in a pathetic army of unintelligent, irresponsible brutes.

In the past, she had tried very hard to love her father, but it was difficult when she completely disagreed with everything he stood for. The man had built an empire on crime and brutality and the more she discovered about his business enterprises, the less she respected him.

It wasn't even that he brought the brutality home. After her mother's death from cancer when she was two, Sierra and her sister had basically been raised by nannies. Her father was negligent at the best of times.

But that one man, with his tall, confident stride, his square jawline and intelligent looking eyes, he'd been different! Surely he couldn't be...

She stopped commiserating her loss when she caught a movement out of the corner of her eye.

Why were three of her father's men walking towards his office? And why the rush?

She stared at the door through which her father and the stranger had disappeared, trying to tell herself not to worry. Something told her to go through that door, to stop...whatever was happening inside that dreaded office. But one of her older cousins chose that moment to come over and tease her about school, obviously trying to distract her from what might be happening.

She kept up the chatter, but her awareness of the ongoing conversation never left her mind. Looking around at the cluster of men surrounding the bar, she didn't like the way they were all watching the door either. It looked like several of them were expecting something dramatic to happen, something that might be hazardous to one's health. Specifically, the health of the man who had disappeared with her father.

But they'd gone into her father's office! That was supposed to be the place he discussed business. She was fairly certain her father didn't condone violence so near to his house. Sierra was under the impression that he maintained a distance from those kinds of activities, even if he might be the man who ordered the violence.

She kept her eye on the doorway to her father's office, wondering if there was some way she could intervene. Maybe if she just pretended to be a ditzy female, stepped in with a silly question for her father, she might catch a glimpse of what was going on inside. Perhaps she could stop anything that could be going wrong? She'd never done something like that before, nor had her father ever allowed her in his office. If he wanted to speak with her, he came to the main house. It was a well-known fact that his office space was forbidden territory. So if she were to do that, his wrath would come down hard on her head.

As she contemplated the situation, she knew that she didn't care what happened to herself. The man that had been lured into her father's office was innocent. She had absolutely no way to know this, but she instinctively knew it was the case. Would her conscience allow her to ignore what might be happening simply because she was afraid of the repercussions?

No. She'd never forgive herself if she didn't do something to stop the brutality despite her shaking hands and rapidly beating, terrified heart.

She stood beside the pool, the heat of the sunshine beating down on her head, as she struggled to come up with a reasonable, or even an unreasonable excuse, for interrupting her father's conference. While she debated the issue, two more of her father's men must have received some sort of signal because both of them started hurrying towards her father's office and Sierra didn't like the looks of things. The two men appeared worried, anxious even and that raised her anxiety level even higher. When these men were anxious, bullets started flying. Their idea of diplomacy was to shoot all moving objects first and sort out the problem later. Dead bodies were merely a hindrance, not a hazard.

She tried to step in front of her father's lieutenants, but her father's second in command, Jimmy, simply stopped her with a hand held out in front of her. She looked up at him, glaring out her anger. "Jimmy, what's going on?" she demanded, trying to hide her terror at the possibilities of what might be happening.

Jimmy was only about two inches taller than she was, but he had an evilness about his eyes that had always made her nervous. He had big, bulky shoulders and a belly that wasn't as bad as some of the others mooching off of her father at the bar, but it definitely would benefit from some abdominal crunches.

Jimmy shook his head. "Nothing you need to worry yourself about, Sierra. Just leave it be," he replied firmly, standing directly in her path and looking as if he were going to stop her if she proceeded to interfere.

Sierra peered around his shoulder, shivering when one of her father's men came out of the house, dunking his now-bloody hand into one of the ice buckets in which the party's beer was cooling. That was the clincher, she thought. There had obviously been violence and it was pretty harsh if the man's hand was any indication. These men prided themselves on dealing with pain inflicted by others, but Tony, the man with his hand in the ice, was not amused by whatever had gone down in the office.

When her father's big, black Lincoln pulled out of the garage, Sierra ignored Jimmy and spun around in the opposite direction. As she rushed through the house, she grabbed her own purse and keys, hurrying out of the house. She raced as quickly as possible through to the garage. She dove into her tiny car, praying she wasn't too late to catch up with the big, black Lincoln. She also fervently prayed that she hadn't been wrong about the handsome stranger being in that car. What if he were still back at the house? What if he needed help and she was off chasing some car with just her father's goons in it heading out for a beer run?

4

As she zipped out of the garage, she spotted the big car turning the corner at the end of the street. She didn't have time to be indecisive. She had to hurry if she was going to catch up with them. She zipped by several of her neighbors, earning a glare for her rude driving and pushed on ahead. She finally caught up with them at the light over by the local grocery store, but held back, afraid her father's men might spot her if she got too close.

Her eyes focused only on keeping up with the huge, black car. She suspected that, somehow, the stranger was inside of that car. Her heart and several pieces of evidence were telling her that something was very, very wrong.

Fifteen minutes later, she stopped a block away from the black car in a relatively dingy, older section of Chicago where the warehouses and now-unused factory buildings were abandoned except for the rats and drug dealers. It was a section that several community groups had tried to revitalize, but without much success. When neither of her father's men got out of the obtrusive vehicle, but a large, dark form was pushed out of the car from the back seat, she gasped in horror.

The black car pulled away with a harsh screeching of tires and Sierra accelerated cautiously forward, her heart pounding frantically with the fear of what she might find.

When she pulled up even with the alleyway, she struggled for breath, shocked by what she was seeing. Sierra jumped out of her car, barely remembering to put it in park in her rush to get to the wounded man laying on the gravel as if he were a piece of trash.

She rushed over to the man, cradling his head in her lap and trying to shield his face from the harsh glare of the sun. She heard him moan and rested her hand against his cheek. "Please don't die on me," she begged to the extremely large, inert form. "You just have to be okay. I'll make this all okay, if you'll just survive this horrible incident," she whispered, unaware that she was actually sobbing out the words.

With her cell phone in one hand, she cradled the man's head, her fingers laying on his cheek as she sobbed almost uncontrollably. She could barely dial nine-one-one because her hand was shaking so badly. As soon as the operator came online she said, "Please, I need an ambulance here as soon as possible."

She squinted into the hot, summer sunshine, trying to read the street signs halfway down the block. It was one of those horrible, hazy days that Chicago was famous for, so the street signs were a bit blurry.

Squinting through the smog, sun and haze, she finally read the words and almost yelled them through the phone. She told the operator her location, and then kept answering the questions about this stranger's condition. She couldn't believe all the bruises that were quickly forming on the man's face and body. His previously pristine, white shirt was now torn and bloodied. As she sat with him, she didn't realize that tears were streaming down her cheeks, inadvertently landing on his face.

When she heard the ambulance in the distance, she felt a small amount of relief. It felt like it had taken them hours to reach her location, but it was probably only minutes. Finally, the paramedics were jumping out of the vehicle with their stretchers and equipment, urging her to step away from the man so they could help him. Sierra didn't want to let go of his head, afraid of letting it rest on the gravel for even a moment. She'd been cradling the man's head in her lap, praying to God that he would save this man from an undeserved death. She had no idea what had gone on in her father's office, but she was sure, with an instinct born of desperation and experience, that this man was innocent. From looking at the condition of the man, he'd probably insulted her father in some way, and this was his punishment.

It wasn't fair. No matter what the insult, no one should have to deal with this kind of torture.

The paramedics were loading the man into the ambulance, telling her to drive to the hospital so she could help her "brother". She didn't understand that part of their comments, but she jumped back into her car and raced behind the ambulance. It took precious moments to find a parking space, but she was racing through the doors of the emergency room entrance just as the stranger was being pushed behind a pair of swinging doors.

"You'll have to wait out here for your brother, ma'am," one of the nurses was telling her, grabbing her arms gently and leading her towards a plastic chair. "He's going to be fine," the woman was assuring her.

"Promise?" Sierra whispered, unaware and uncaring that the tears were falling once again – unconcerned that she had mascara streaks on her cheeks and her brown, curly hair was sticking out in different directions. She even had some of the man's blood on her own shirt. It would ruin the blouse, but that was inconsequential compared to the man's pain and anguish. She just wanted that man to live.

"The doctors at this facility are excellent," the woman assured Sierra, resting a firm hand on her shoulder. "They will do everything to help him. You can be sure of that."

Sierra didn't like that statement. It wasn't the absolute reassurance that she was looking for, but more of an anemic comment that nurses all around the world made to people who were panicking about their loved one.

She had no idea how long she sat in the painful, plastic chair, staring at the double doors, watching people rush in and out, doctors going in but not coming out. She lost count of how many doctors were trying to heal the man. On one level, she should be reassured that so much expertise was being expended. On the other hand, she didn't like the possibility that he was so hurt that he needed that much care.

It might have been an hour or ten, she wasn't really sure. There weren't any windows where she was sitting so she wouldn't have been able to gauge the time even if her mind were functioning enough to make the connection between the daylight and nighttime. In fact, she must have fallen asleep because the next thing she knew, a gentle hand was touching her shoulder. Sierra jerked awake with a start. It took her only seconds to realize where she was and she jumped up, ignoring the shooting pain in her legs that had been curled up in the tiny, uncomfortable, plastic chair for what might have been several hours.

"Yes?" Sierra felt the shivering start even before the doctor had a chance to explain. "Is he okay? Is he in pain?"

The doctor smiled into her soft, blue eyes, relieved that he could convey good news this time. "Your brother is going to be okay," he said to reassure her.

Sierra felt as if she were going to faint with that news but she gripped the back of the chair and forced her mind to function properly. As the news sunk in, she was so relieved, she started crying again, grabbing the doctor's hand and gripping it between both of hers. "Thank you!" she whispered with intensity.

"Not so fast," the doctor cautioned gently, clearing his throat at the stunningly beautiful woman standing before him. Even with her mascara running down her face, he could see her porcelain complexion. Her big, blue eyes made him forget his wife while she looked up at him. They actually made him forget to breathe for a moment. This young girl was exquisitely gorgeous and the deep compassion shining through her lovely eyes only added to her beauty.

He felt bad when those blue eyes filled up with anxiety. The doctor shook his head and focused on her words, trying to explain the whole situation. He had to stop thinking of her loveliness and focus on explaining her brother's condition.

Clearing his throat, he took her hand and guided her back to the chairs so they were both sitting down. "He's going to need a great deal of care. Right now, he's in a coma so that," he heard her gasp but put a reassuring hand to her shoulder and guided her back to focus on his words, " so we could operate more safely. He has several broken ribs, one of which punctured a lung. His right collar bone is broken, his left leg is broken in two places and there are several contusions which bruised his internal organs. Thankfully, nothing was punctured or things would have been much worse. But it was a good thing you were right there and able to call when you did. He wouldn't have made it if you'd been any later." The doctor chuckled at the young beauty's worried expression. "That was some bar fight he was in."

Sierra absorbed all of this information with a painful heart. The doctor thought the man had been in a bar fight? Should she tell him the truth? What would happen if she said that her father's men had done this? Surely there would still be blood in her father's office. Maybe the police could seize the car and have it tested. But would that get back to his father? He hadn't been driving the car, she hadn't seen him beat up this stranger and she hadn't even heard him order the beating.

Or was her father smart enough to clean up all the evidence? He wasn't a stupid man. No one could create the enormous criminal empire Joe Berutelli commanded and be unintelligent. He'd gone this long without any problems with the law, or at least no problems that she knew about, so it was probably a good bet that he'd already cleaned up any evidence that might incriminate him.

Besides, if she told this doctor that it hadn't been a bar fight, the police would get involved and they might start asking questions. If they asked anything of her father, he would know that the stranger was still alive.

Wasn't it better to let the man heal before she took on gaining justice for the stranger?

A moment later, the doctor cleared his throat and looked serious again so Sierra brought her eyes up from the floor to focus on his kind features once again. "He's in recovery now and the medicine we used to induce the coma will be wearing off pretty soon. He'll be moved to the intensive care unit and I can't say how long it will take before he recovers enough to be moved to a regular room, much less to be released." He looked sad as he said, "This could be a long, painful and expensive ordeal ahead for your brother."

"Don't worry about payment. I'll make sure everything is taken care of. Just make sure he's not in any pain. Please!" Sierra cried, relieved that he was still alive. She'd take it one day at a time. "When can I see him?" she asked, not sure if the beaten man even wanted to see her but she could peek at him while he was unconscious, just to make sure he was really okay.

The doctor smiled, blushing slightly when Sierra smiled back at him. Embarrassed at his reaction since he was a fifty year old man and this woman couldn't be older than twenty, he admonished himself and reminded himself of his mission at the moment. Besides, she was probably younger than twenty by the kind, innocent look about her.

As the doctor glanced around, he noticed several other men in the waiting room were having the same problem and he instinctively wanted to put a protective wall around this girl-child, to guard her against their lascivious thoughts. He hated the way several of the men were glancing in her direction, some of them actually staring with adoration.

In answer to her question, he said, "He'll be brought to the ICU as soon as the nurses in the recovery room think that he is well enough to endure the change. Once he's set up, the nurses will allow you to talk to him. Whatever you say, be positive, talk to him, let him hear your voice so he knows that his family is around him, reassure him that everything is going to be okay and tell him stories of his past or about your other brothers and sisters. We don't know all that happens with the brain, but we know that he will hear your voice and recognize what you're telling him."

"Yes!" she gasped, excited about the doctor's prognosis and eager to help in any way possible. "I'll go down there right now."

She was grabbing her purse as the doctor walked wearily down the hallway when one of the nurses stopped her. "Miss?" she called out.

Sierra stopped hurrying, trying to smile but she was too tired at this point, and too relieved. All she wanted to do was to see this stranger and make sure that her father hadn't damaged him too much. "Yes?" she asked.

"I'm sorry to bring this up at this point, but we need your brother's insurance information," the nurse said, handing the forms on a clipboard to Sierra.

Sierra had no idea if the man had health insurance or not, but she wasn't going to impose the expense of her father's brutality on the man's financial woes. Pulling out her wallet, she slipped a credit card out of the slot. "Here, use this for any expenses," she said, knowing that her father hadn't put any limit on this credit card. It would serve him right to pay for the recovery of the man he'd beaten. "Don't spare any expense to help this man get better," Sierra urged the nurse who was looking back at her with a surprised expression.

"But don't you want..." she started to say, only to stop when Sierra shook her head adamantly.

"No. All expenses should go on that card. If the card won't cover it, contact me immediately and I'll make sure everything is paid for," she said, writing down her contact information. She would sell the jewelry her father had given her over the years in order to pay the man's hospital expenses if the credit card wouldn't cover all the costs.

With that, Sierra walked away, furious with her father and shaking with anticipation at seeing the stranger she'd never actually met. Their eyes had seen each other, but she was sure he wouldn't remember her. There had been too much going on at the party for him to have really seen her so she'd have to be careful. She didn't want him to recognize her since it might bring back bad memories.

She followed the directions to the ICU and was finally directed to the correct room. She found the man lying on the hospital bed hooked up to so many machines her stomach twisted into knots just hearing their beeping noises.

She was amazed because, even with bruises covering his face, bandages around his head and around his chest, his leg encased in a cast and so many machines beeping around him, the man still managed to look amazingly sexy and confident. She stepped into the room, her fingers tenderly touching his hand as she sat down in the chair. "I'm so sorry," she whispered, looking at the man's features in an effort to see if he understood anything she'd said. "I can't believe my father did this to you, but I'll try very hard to make it right."

She told him what the doctor had said, commenting on how nice he looked, how handsome he had seemed when he'd first stepped out onto the patio and how he had taken her breath away. She kept talking to him, fearful that one of the nurses would tell her that she had to leave or that visiting hours were finished. But no one disturbed her although occasionally someone came in to check on the man's vitals or to put something into the IV.

The morning sun was just starting to creep over the horizon but she ignored the time and her exhaustion. The nurse came in at some point, smiled at Sierra and urged her to keep talking because it was "helping enormously". Apparently, the man's vitals were extremely strong for someone in his condition. There was a worry about infection, but Sierra promised to be careful, not sure if she could do anything to stop an infection, but willing to do anything to try.

She had no concept of time, just of the man's features as he valiantly tried to recover from his injuries. She held his hand, her fingers rubbing his bruised and bloodied knuckles, surprised at the calluses on his fingers and the palm of his hand. It indicated that he was a working man. The complete opposite of what she had thought upon first seeing him. That only made him more attractive to her and she wanted to comfort him. His calluses and his dress shirt were a contradiction. The shirt was obviously expensive, but his hand indicated a completely different lifestyle. She liked even the mystery about him.

As she stared at his handsome, beaten and bruised face, her thoughts drifted to what he might be like as a person. She wanted to kiss him, to run her fingers through his hair and feel the softness. Or would his hair be rough like his hands? His chest was so muscular and she blushed when one of the nurses stepped in to check his bandages, revealing the man's stomach which was ridged with muscles, just as she'd suspected when she'd seen him across the pool. What she hadn't anticipated was the enticing line of black hair that curled up from below the stiff hospital sheet. Very intriguing, she thought as she tried to hide her interest from the nurses.

Was he naked below? She shivered at the idea and then pushed it aside. The man was in a coma! How could she even think something like that? She'd never seen a naked man but here she was, trying to get a peek at him.

As soon as they were alone once again, she turned back to the man, a grimace on her face. She knew he couldn't see it so she felt a little silly. "Sorry about my bad thoughts," she whispered to him. "I have to confess that you're a very fascinating specimen of manhood. But that's really no excuse because you're...well," she blushed and looked at the man from the top of his head to his toes that were sticking out of his cast, "you're incapacitated and that's not really fair."

"I'll confess that I haven't really dated anyone seriously and even those boys that I've dated, well, they're no match to you physically. Not that you would be even remotely interested in me because I'm well…I'm me," she said, thinking about her breasts, or lack of breasts. She laughed, feeing ridiculous, but she couldn't move away. She was drawn to this man in some odd, indefinable way. "I'm afraid I'm taking advantage of you by looking at your body when you're not around to tell me to stop. I know I'd feel very angry if our positions were reversed." She thought about that for a moment, looking down at his long, elegant fingers, the skin over his knuckles broken and battered which gave her a smile because the man had fought back, at least for a few minutes. "Anyway," she laughed and moved her fingers higher on his hand, covering his wrist and feeling the strong bones underneath her fingers, "I shouldn't be so fascinated but I am and you're asleep so I'll at least pretend that I'm ashamed of my lack of consideration."

She sighed and ran her fingers over his forearm, loving the almost rough feel of the arm on his skin. It was so different from her own skin and she was completely entranced by the differences.

"Okay, I'll behave," she promised, but it was only a half-hearted attempt at being appropriate. She laughed softly and shook her head. "At least, I'll try to behave. It isn't easy since you are extremely fascinating." She glanced at his face, so bruised and battered and her heart broke for his pain. "Probably not something you want to hear right now, though. I'm sorry. You're probably thinking I'm totally insensitive. And you'd be correct." She looked at him with soft eyes. "My only excuse is that, well, confidentially, you're quite spellbinding. I don't believe I've ever met anyone quite like you." She grimaced again. "Not that we've actually met. Not officially, anyway. Nor will we ever meet. You'll probably hate me if you knew who I was." She was rambling now, but the doctor had said he could hear her so she shifted to other, more interesting subjects.

She continued to talk to him until her voice was hoarse and she couldn't speak any longer. She wasn't sure when it happened, but she fell asleep, her head resting against his hip and her hand holding his own.

Drake woke up at some point in the night, confused and in more pain than he'd ever thought was possible. He couldn't move his leg and he slowly lifted his head in order to figure out why but even that was difficult. His leg was encased in a cast and lifted higher than the bed on some sort of pulley system. There were beeping sounds all around him, lights, white sheets, a hideous mint colored wall…he was in the hospital, he finally realized.

His face hurt like hell and he tried to lift his hand to figure out why but he couldn't move his arm, which confused him. Nothing about his arm hurt. His ribs hurt, it ached to breathe, there was something seriously wrong with his stomach and he couldn't believe the pain shooting up both of his legs. But nothing was wrong with his arm except that he couldn't move it.

He laid his head on the scratchy hospital pillow, every cell in his brain aching with the pain shooting around in his skull. When he finally had enough energy, he lifted his head once again and looked at his arm and was startled to find the dark-haired beauty he'd seen earlier today. Or was it yesterday? He wasn't sure what day it was, or even if it was day or night.

She was laying on his arm, her hair draped over his thigh with the curls wrapping around in places he really shouldn't be thinking about right now.

He suddenly realized that she'd been crying. He wanted to lift his hand, to touch the tear tracks that had marred that beautiful skin but she was holding his hand tightly and he couldn't move anything. In the end, he accepted that it felt good to just have her close, to smell that incredible, honeysuckle perfume, and listen to her soft breathing.

He closed his eyes, intending to rest for just a moment, but by the time he opened his eyes again, the woman was gone, replaced by a stern looking nurse who was trying to take his pulse.

"So you're awake?" the nurse asked, her eyes assessing him carefully. Without even a smile, she wrote something on a paper attached to a clip board and walked out. "I'll inform the doctor," she said and she was gone. He wasn't sure if his need for information was stronger than his fear of her harsh demeanor. He wanted to understand what was going on, but that nurse was a tough cookie and he wasn't sure he could butt heads with her right now. Maybe later, he promised himself.

He slept fitfully for what seemed like a long time. Every once in a while, he dreamed that he was walking through the forest, surrounded by honeysuckle and he breathed in the scent, enjoying the calming effect it had on his pain. Every time he smelled her, his body ached just a little bit less.

Several times, he thought he heard her talking to him, telling him stories about…school? No, not possible. But she was giving him arguments for taking calculus and linear algebra, something about discrete mathematics and numerical analysis. Was she actually giving him the pros for statistics? No one liked statistics, he thought but his mouth was still too sore to actually form the words, and he couldn't even open his eyes to let her know that he heard her. He smiled though. Well, at least he thought he was smiling. She certainly liked discussing math.

Drake liked math, could do complex problems in his mind, but he didn't enjoy math simply for the challenge of doing math problems, which is what he suspected she enjoyed. He used math as a tool, something to further his business efforts and gain the competitive edge over his rivals.

Finally, he wasn't sure if it was hours or days, he was able to open his eyes, to look around and the pain was…well, it was still bad, but it was at least bearable.

Unfortunately, his little brunette beauty wasn't by his side. Standing beside him was that same nurse as the last time he'd woken. Had he only been dreaming about the other woman? Had she been a figment of his imagination?

Surely not. The scent, the voice…he knew he'd heard her. And he'd felt her soft hair. It had been curling around his wrist and floating on top of his hip. He hadn't seen her face, but he was sure that she'd been real.

"Where's the woman?" he asked, his voice scratchy from lack of use and his eyes felt as if they were barely open. Were his eyes swollen for some reason? He tried to think back, to figure out why he was here in the hospital. But he was more focused on trying to figure out where the soft-haired woman was. He needed her. He desperately wanted to hear her soft voice, to laugh at her debates about math classes and find out what she'd finally decided to do about school.

The nurse shot him a curious look, still not smiling. "Your sister?" she asked, again pausing to write something on the chart at the end of his bed.

"Don't have a sister," he croaked out. "The beautiful one. The one that smells good."

He could have sworn the nurse actually cracked a smile, but then she turned stern once again. "Only family is allowed in during visiting hours," she stated firmly.

Drake closed his eyes again, but he wasn't going to sleep through her next visit.

Unfortunately, she never came again. He stayed awake as much as possible but he never saw her return to his side. He asked about her to the nurses and doctors, but all of them gave him the same answer; thin, blue eyes and brown hair. He knew that couldn't completely describe her and it was almost an obsession to find her, get more information on her.

He spent half of his mental capabilities on devising a plan to get back at the man who had done this to him, and the other half trying to figure out who his mystery woman was. His construction business didn't falter during his hospitalization, mainly due to the fact that he'd hired many very good employees and they were fully capable of continuing the work on the multiple projects that he had going on across the country. But he wouldn't let the woman or his retribution leave his mind.

A month after he arrived at the hospital, he was allowed to leave, but with strict instructions on visiting his own doctor or coming back to the hospital for a follow up with his surgeon. He could get the cast off in another two weeks as long as he kept as much of his weight off of it as possible, using the crutches whenever he could. "I'm sure my health insurance is going to skyrocket with this little sojourn," he said to the nurse as she helped him dress.

The nurse quickly shook her head. "Your entire bill has been paid in full along with a deposit in case you need any other medical assistance because of this accident."

Drake looked at the nurse strangely. "Who paid all the expenses?" he asked, knowing that the cost would be huge. A month in a hospital, including the long period in which he was in intensive care, wouldn't be cheap by anyone's budget.

"The woman we all thought was your sister. She was here all the time that first week, sitting outside your room when she wasn't allowed in. Every day, she was interrogating the doctors to make sure you were getting everything you needed, bringing us cookies and brownies, or just dropping off some flowers. I think those were all bribes just to convince us take better care of you," she joked with a wink as she helped him lower himself into the wheel chair. His leg was still in a cast and several of his ribs were too tender for crutches so he'd be in a wheel chair for a couple more weeks. "You have a very good friend out there. Of course, if we'd known she wasn't your sister, we wouldn't have let her into the intensive care room." She thought about it for a moment, then shrugged. "Or maybe we would have. Your vitals definitely were better when she was sitting next to you, holding your hand."

His foreman and best friend was standing outside the room, ready to bring Drake home for the first time in thirty days. Drake wanted to ask the nurse more, to get a description of the woman he only knew was beautiful with dark, brown hair and tender eyes. He didn't even remember what color her eyes were, only that they were filled with compassion and hope. Her image had gotten him through the worst of the pain and the hope of seeing her each time he woke up had pushed him to recover more quickly.

When Tony stepped in again, he had a grim expression on his face. "Ready?" he asked.

That reminded him of his plans. Joe Berutelli had done this. He'd remembered the questions, the demands from the shorter man to take bribes, to use different vendors – vendors Drake knew distributed cheaper, inferior materials. Those materials wouldn't hold up under the long term use of any building and could cause injuries. There had been an argument that afternoon in the man's office and Drake had stood firm, refusing to relinquish his good name despite ominous threats of chaos and brutality to himself, his family and his workers if he didn't cooperate with the organized crime gang. After Berutelli had accepted that Drake wasn't going to play ball, the beating had started.

There had been three goons roughing him up at first. But when Drake was winning, tossing the guys off of him and knocking them out, two more guys showed up, this time with bats. That had been the end of his ability to fight them off. He'd gone down, feeling every punch and smack of the wooden bat.

Drake looked up at his friend, fury raging through his mind now that he was going home. "Absolutely. We have a lot of work to do. Namely, take down one mafia boss," he replied. "And I'm going to enjoy every moment of this."

Tony shook his head. "Why don't we just leave things as is?" he suggested nervously. They had been in the middle of a huge construction job when he'd received word that Drake had been badly beaten and was in the hospital. They all knew who had done it, but Joe Berutelli had come up with a perfect alibi, claiming he had been hosting a party at the time of the attack with numerous witnesses who said that Joe had never left, and also that Drake had left on his own two feet. So the police couldn't do anything about it.

Drake shook his head, rolling himself out of the room simply because he could now. He had just finished a period in his life when he'd been almost completely incapacitated. He wouldn't let that happen again. "I can't let this go, Tony. And don't worry about anything. I have this all figured out," he assured the older man.

Elizabeth Lennox

CHAPTER 1

Six years later...

Drake watched with fascination as the woman in the pencil skirt shifted to a different angel, her body bent over the architect's drafting board and providing him with a very enticing view. It wasn't so much the woman's concentration or the fact that she was humming softly to herself. It was the way she was almost dancing with her sexy skirt pulled against her very cute, very round derriere, her long legs ending with pretty shoes that made her legs look even longer, showing off her slender, muscular calves. Every few moments, her bottom would wiggle as she hit a high note on whatever song was going through her headphones.

He tried to listen to the notes in order to decipher the song, but she only sang a few lines, then danced or wiggled again while the song continued in her head.

He could tell that she had dark brown, shiny hair that curled softly at the ends but, besides her great legs and adorable butt, there wasn't anything else he could see of the woman. Even her hair was pulled back into an elaborate twist on the back of her head. It looked feminine and professional, but gave nothing away.

He watched her, enjoying the view for several moments, only cringing a few times during her song when she really missed a note. Her lack of ability to sing well didn't diminish his capacity to enjoy the view. It was just too interesting to tear his eyes away.

"Sorry about that," Todd said, coming around the corner of the hallway, slightly out of breath as he hurried to catch up. Zeke pushed away from the door frame, acting as if he hadn't just been ogling one of his newest employees.

Drake almost laughed when the woman in question jumped and spun around so she was now facing her visitors. She was so startled, her hand jerked in the air, causing her pen to flip from her hand, flying through the air while her arms suddenly flailed out in surprise in a vain attempt to intersect the tiny missile. She quickly grabbed the edge of her work table to steady herself, but not in time. Her feet tripped over each other and she had to reach out and grab the back of her office chair to steady herself.

Drake stared, amazed that a woman as stunning and sexy as this actually existed. And that she was so amazingly clumsy. She was, in a word, perfect. Her blue eyes shimmered with embarrassment coloring her high cheekbones that quickly changed from creamy porcelain to a soft, becoming peach color.

He almost groaned as he looked at her fully. Her figure wasn't just enticing from behind. She had luscious breasts that pushed against the crisp, navy suit that tried valiantly to contain them as well as slender hips that continued down to long, slender legs. The entire package was impressive and immediately caused his mind to wander to completely inappropriate ideas.

Todd went on as if nothing were happening, entirely unaware of the electricity sparking between the two other people in the room. "Have you had a chance to meet Sierra? She's one of the best architects I've ever had the pleasure of working with. She's creative, innovative and has great ideas on how to incorporate green concepts into structures without degrading quality or increasing price."

Drake already knew all this, but he'd been expecting someone much older. Sierra Colbert was an up-and-coming architect. She was becoming well known for her work, but there weren't any pictures of her, since she didn't use the conference or speaking circuit like so many others did to increase their exposure.

Who knew she was a knockout on top of being a brilliant architect?

Drake nodded, indicating that he'd done his homework and was familiar with her ideas.

Todd continued on, extolling Sierra's previous designs and embarrassing her further. "She's done some great work lately." Turning to Sierra he said, "Can you show him the designs you did for that project over in Seattle for the Hutton Foundation?" Todd asked.

When she finally got her heart rate back down from the surprise, she looked at the man that had been on her mind almost every day for the past six years. She couldn't believe he was actually here, actually in her office and his presence literally knocked the breath out of her lungs, she was so excited.

Sierra's initial reaction had been surprise, immediately followed by recognition and then excitement. Drake Hamilton was here? He was okay and he looked fabulously vibrant! The years had been good to him and he looked healthier now than he had that first day at her father's pool party. She couldn't believe that she'd actually run into him again.

She'd followed his career over the past six years, impressed with his ability to grow his construction and real estate company into a global enterprise. His services were asked for above all other construction firms because he was ethical, creative and almost always came in under budget.

His company didn't simply build corporate headquarters around the globe. This man created cities! When he took on a project, there wasn't just the main building. He would design the whole area around the building, generating a community that would thrive even if the company went out of business. It was a new concept in construction and real estate, one that had been impossible to conceive of ten years ago. Drake's business had pioneered the concept and she thought he was brilliant because of it.

Then it occurred to her what was actually happening. Drake Harrison was here? He was here! No! He couldn't be here! The two of them were never supposed to meet. Her excitement quickly diminished, swallowed up by the fear that he might recognize her. And if he connected her with her father, what might he do? How would he react?

She'd thought about this man for so long, she hadn't ever imagined actually meeting him. And she couldn't imagine what he would do if he realized who she was, who her father was.

And then something completely different hit her. She looked at the man she'd known six years ago for less than a month, a month in which he had been completely incapacitated. There was something about the way he was looking at her, something that made her feel...vulnerable? Why was he looking at her like that? It was almost as if he considered her to be his next meal.

An instant tug of awareness struck her but she brutally suppressed the sensation. She couldn't permit herself to think like that, to have feelings for the man. At least not...those...feelings. No, Drake Harrison was definitely off limits in all ways – and being drawn to him was an absolute no no.

Todd had stopped speaking and the stranger was waiting to shake her hand.

Realizing that the man was waiting for a response, she sputtered out a greeting as quickly as possible. "It's a pleasure to meet you," she lied, extending her hand. Well, it wasn't a complete lie. She was thrilled that he was so healthy and vital, so...okay, so no other word for it, the man was hot!

But he wasn't supposed to be here! Why was he here? He's supposed to be in Chicago!

Drake looked at her soft, elegant hand and took it in his larger one, swallowing up her pale hand and feeling the shock as he looked into her pretty, blue eyes. He felt her start to tremble and every instinct inside of him wanted to pull her into his arms and kiss her, tell her that everything was going to be okay and she didn't need to be frightened of him.

There was something about this woman that struck him deeply. Something that told him that she was going to be his, no matter what it took to convince her. Even the possibility that he would need to convince any woman was a foreign concept to him. Women tended to be embarrassingly obvious, sometimes obnoxiously aggressive, in their interest.

So why was this woman trying to pull her hand away from his? He could see that she was interested, felt her pulse with his fingertips as he shook her hand. He wanted to pull her close, ask her questions, find out what made her tick. But it seemed that all she wanted to do was run away and hide.

No, he almost chuckled out loud. That wasn't the way this was going to go down. He looked at her stunning features, keeping his eyes on hers as he planned out his seduction. He instantly knew that he wanted this woman. He wanted her badly. Why she was pulling away, he didn't understand, but very soon, he would know all her secrets. In fact, he planned to be one of them!

Sierra glared at the man, her excitement at seeing him so healthy fading as her awareness of him as a man, a very large, very muscular and, apparently, very arrogant man increased and scared her. Why wouldn't he release her hand? Why was he drawing this out? Couldn't he understand that she wanted space? She hated arrogant men.

Didn't she?

So why was her stomach fluttering? Why was she having a hard time catching her breath? It definitely wasn't because this man's touch was firing her blood.

Actually, she'd never been around arrogant men. Most of the men she ran into were soft and flabby. They would never impose on her personal space if she sent the right signals. And she was definitely sending the "stay away" signals to Mr. Harrison, so why wasn't he backing up? Why wasn't he giving her the breathing room she needed? She felt flustered, irritated and…yep, there was that word again: vulnerable.

No, she was just nervous about meeting strangers. She wasn't a good people pleaser, not able to play the political office games well. She preferred to stay in the background, do her work and enjoy the thrill of watching her buildings come to life. She enjoyed speaking with her clients, but generally left the glad-handing to Todd and the others.

She tried once again to get her hand free, but he only held onto her hand more tightly, his other hand actually coming up to cover hers, trapping her fingers in his large palm with the roughened calluses that had always seemed so sexy when she'd held his hand before.

Why wouldn't he release her hand? Unless she wanted to have an embarrassing tug of war, she had to just stand here and endure his irritating touch while Todd droned on about her accomplishments, going into awkward details about her ideas and how they'd been implemented on various projects.

When her hand was finally free, she took a deep, calming breath and looked down. She suddenly remembered the designs Todd had mentioned she should show to Drake Harrison and jumped on that as an easy excuse to step back slightly. She bent low over a cabinet to find the file. "Here's the file Todd mentioned. I'll just leave this with you and if you have any questions, feel free to give me a call. I'm sure you've seen much more impressive designs from your more experienced architects and designers. This might be a bit of a letdown from what you're used to," she replied, desperately wishing Todd would stop talking and this man would just walk away. She felt like she needed an ice pack to recover from the heat stealing up her arm after his touch. The whole episode had probably lasted seconds but to her befuddled mind, it seemed like hours, hours upon which she didn't understand why Todd couldn't see the tension, couldn't sense her nervousness.

"On the contrary," his deep voice countered. "I've heard about you and thought your work was excellent. I'm eager to work with you."

"Work" with her? Why would he be working with her, or any of the architects in this firm? He was one of the big guys. He was the one that set the standard in the industry. Todd's firm took on national projects, but most of their efforts were very small, very niche oriented.

Sierra's startled glance pulled away from his dark eyes and glanced over at her boss. "I don't think I can take on another client right now," she said to Todd, nerves coming out as she frantically tried to think of a way to avoid working too closely with this man. She needed to be as far away from him as possible. For so many reasons! "I have four houses in various stages of completion at the moment."

It was no longer just about him discovering who she was, but that was definitely a part of it. With Todd's words, her new worry was more about working closely, spending long hours with this man to discuss his project needs. She spent hours discussing a project with her clients, ensuring that she captured exactly what they wanted in their home or office space. She didn't want to do that with this man.

There was something about this man that, in Sierra's mind, made him dangerous on a more personal level. She had no idea how she knew that, but something inside of her told her that he wasn't the kind of man who would be satisfied with a chaste kiss at the end of the night.

Now why would she think about kissing him when he was simply going to be a client?

Her eyes accidentally moved to his lips and her breath caught in the back of her throat. She thought she might have gasped as her eyes took in his firm lips that were smiling slightly. Her mind immediately jumped to what those lips would feel like…on other places of her body instead of just her mouth.

What?! How had she gone from not wanting to work with him, to not wanting to kiss him and…? Where in the world had that come from? She could feel her face flaming and took a deep breath to calm herself down.

Focus, Sierra! This man was not interested in a date! He was a potential client. She never dated any of her clients! She barely even went out to lunch with them unless it was the only time she could get answers on questions. End of project celebrations? Yes, certainly. But that included the whole staff who had worked on the project.

No dating! No kissing! And definitely no…other things!

She hated the way she felt when he looked down at her. It was almost as if he could read her mind and those firm lips actually broadened into a grin as her mind raced frantically to inappropriate thoughts. That heart-racing, tummy-tightening, mind numbing feeling made her want to sprint out of the office, to hide somewhere safe. Some place where his striking eyes couldn't make her feel as if he were looking at her naked. And liking what he saw!

Todd was still talking about her accomplishments and Sierra finally was able to tear her eyes away from the new guy and focus on what her boss was saying. "Take a look at that file and you'll get an idea of what she can do. I think she's definitely the person you're looking for that could add a great deal of value to the projects you're considering."

Sierra looked at her boss, a man she'd respected intensely for years. He'd mentored her through some complex work and given her more opportunities than she would have received if she'd gone with any other firm. But why was he asking her to show this man her work? Not this man. Anyone but this particular man.

Memories of him laying in a hospital bed, his body broken and bruised because of her father's cruelty, came rushing through her mind. If Drake Harrison ever found out that she was related to the man who had almost killed him, who had actually left him for dead, he would hate her with an intensity that didn't bear considering.

Everything was so confusing! She didn't like the many paths her mind kept jumping onto. She didn't understand and confusion was difficult to deal with. Add in her emotional reaction as well as the physical response and she was just all over the place mentally!

Deciding to ask a few questions that might give her fried brain some much needed answers, she cleared her throat and squeezed her "frustration ball" behind her back. "I'm sorry," she interrupted as smoothly as possible under the circumstances. "But what's going on?" she asked, glancing nervously between her boss and the man who justifiably should hate her.

Drake raised an eyebrow, wondering why she was asking that question. An e-mail had gone out to all employees informing them of the acquisition this morning.

He and Todd had been wandering the hallways, going from office to office, meeting each person, answering questions and generally just being visible in order to reassure everyone that things wouldn't change with the new management.

Todd chuckled, obviously understanding the situation. "You have that big presentation this morning, don't you?" He'd worked with Sierra for too long not to see the signs. "Did you even go home last night?" he asked, wondering if she'd spent the night working on the details in order to perfect any issues she'd perceived in her work. She'd done it before and he'd admonished her for it, but Sierra was one of those employees that took on a challenge and didn't stop until she'd corrected any issues. Her dedication was one of the reasons clients asked for her so often.

Sierra squeezed the ball behind her once again, knowing that with each squeeze, the ball's "eyes" would bug out, keeping hers from doing the same. "Yes," she replied as if she didn't understand how the two questions were related.

Todd smiled patiently. "This is Drake Harrison. He's took over the firm as of last night at midnight. You would know that if you'd taken the time to read your e-mail this morning before you dove into your work." Todd looked at her over the top of his glasses, his message both amused because he knew that she'd probably put in too many hours of overtime recently, and slightly admonishing because he'd told her several times over the years to check her e-mail every morning before she became too absorbed in her work. "Everyone was informed about three hours ago. There's a big luncheon in the main conference room in two hours to get to know Mr. Harrison better. Will you be there?"

Sierra was about to decline, not wanting to be around when the extremely tall, now-healthy and somewhat terrifying Drake Harrison decided to do his meet and greet. The less time she was around him, the less chance he had of recognizing her and the less time she had to experience this disconcerting reaction her body had to his nearness.

She looked from Todd to the stranger who really wasn't a stranger, wanting desperately to hide somewhere.

"Um...I wasn't..."

Drake could see where this was going and he wasn't going to let her off the hook. She was fascinating, he thought while he watched the expressions change on her lovely features as she tried to get out of the meeting. "She'll be there," he contradicted before she could even decline the invitation.

She blinked and looked up at the man's blue eyes. "I will?"

She took a deep breath, trying to remember that she should be thrilled that Mr. Harrison was so vital and healthy. He'd come such a long way and he'd been laid low by some cruel men but had persevered. In her mind, she knew she should be celebrating his health.

Unfortunately, confronted by him now with that arrogance on his handsome features, and with him standing here telling her what she was going to do when he clearly knew that she didn't want to attend the luncheon, something snapped inside of her.

She turned to fully face him, her eyebrows going up in inquiry. "I didn't know I was going to attend. What time was I going to attend?"

Todd started to interject but Drake stepped forward, looking down at her and doing his best to intimidate her. "You're going to be there at noon, just like the message stated." He waited a long moment, daring her to ignore the summons.

Sierra kept her mouth shut. Her initial reaction was to tell him to go to hell. But Todd had just explained that this was her new boss. Telling off one's boss in the first two minutes after meeting him would be a pretty bad career move. But she couldn't simply accept his summons meekly. That simply wasn't in her coding.

She actually squirmed slightly under his steady, challenging gaze. Was he daring her for some reason? She tried to look meek and mild but it irked her too deeply that he was doing this to her.

If only she hadn't felt the heat in his hand when he'd touched her a moment ago. If only he hadn't felt that shiver go through her whole body as he'd looked down at her.

"I really need to get these plans finalized for a meeting in thirty minutes," she replied, not committing to being at the lunch but not blatantly ignoring the summons either. At least not in his presence.

Drake watched the younger woman's features and knew that she was going to skip the lunch. He wanted to laugh at her bravery but he was having too hard of a time controlling his body's urges to pull her into his arms and kiss her until she obeyed the summons. Or maybe simply because she was going to defy him.

He enjoyed her blush though. And the way she gripped the table behind her. All little signs that she was completely aware of him, just as he was very aware of her as well.

So be it, he thought silently. The gauntlet had been tossed and he had never been one to ignore a challenge.

"I'll see you later then," he replied.

Sierra nodded her head, but she was so tense, it probably came out as simply a snobbish tilt instead. When he finally turned around and walked to the next office, she let out the breath she hadn't even known she'd been holding. With great, heaving breaths, she took in air and tried to cool herself down.

What had just happened? She turned back to her drafting board, wanting to put him out of her mind and just dive back into the safe and benign world of lines and calculations. She understood angles and math. She understood the solid materials that would support a building in different ways and for various reasons.

She didn't understand Drake Harrison.

As she stared down at her work, she realized that she'd only created her fantasy man in her head. The man who had been laying in the hospital bed, fighting for his life, hadn't been able to speak so she'd made up a personality for him. She'd been safe from the real man. Safe from who he might actually be.

But now that she'd met him, she didn't understand why he affected her like this. Men had never impacted her in such a way that she couldn't think or act appropriately and professionally. She'd never thought about any of her dates in such a sexual way. And except for her first crush in high school, she couldn't remember ever blushing when in the presence of another man.

She shook her head, remembering that she had a meeting in just a few minutes. She didn't have time to contemplate the inner workings of the real life man or her reaction to him. It wasn't that he hadn't lived up to her fantasies. It was more that she didn't like what happened to her when he came close. She hadn't expected that reaction. And she definitely didn't like it. She'd felt vulnerable. Exposed.

She'd endured that feeing with her father for years although she knew she couldn't honestly compare what she'd felt while living in her father's house to what she felt when Drake Harrison stepped close to her. There was vulnerability yes, but the feelings were completely different. With her father, there had always been the threat of violence and anger. With Drake, there was...something else. Like he knew all of her secret desires. Things even she didn't want to acknowledge about herself.

Unfortunately, her eyes didn't see the lines and the details of this man like she understood a building's layout. All she saw was his face, his amused eyes as if he were fully aware that she was lying about attending the lunch with all of the other staff members.

She wanted to growl at her confused emotions. What she was feeling was completely out of character. She was a good employee and she tried very hard to be a compassionate person. But that man banished all of her efforts in both of those areas and, it seemed, eliminated her common sense.

This man terrified her on several levels. She didn't see recognition in his eyes, not that he would have any reason to recognize her. He'd been unconscious almost the entire time she'd stayed with him. When he'd finally regained consciousness in the hospital after over a week in the intensive care unit, she'd made sure that his foreman or someone else was there to be with him. She'd kept tabs on him, but also kept her distance, not wanting him to realize who she was or why she was there.

She'd paid all of his medical bills anonymously, even selling her jewelry when her father cut off her credit card after he'd realized what she'd done. She hadn't cared at all about the jewelry. He'd bought it for her to show her off. In his mind, his children wearing expensive jewelry was a status symbol. So selling it made a statement in her own mind. It was a rejection of his life; the proceeds used to rectify the wrongs he'd committed, at least in Drake Harrison's case.

Adding to her defiance, she'd moved out of her father's house that week, not even telling him. He'd said some horrible things about her sister Marissa, things Sierra had been unable to ignore. So she'd just left.

When her father had gone to prison the following year, she hadn't even attended the trial, relieved that someone had finally found enough evidence to convict him and several of his underlings. She'd gone with the assumption that her father was guilty of everything he was accused of and more. So much more! In fact, if she'd been able to find evidence of his crimes, she would have turned it over to the police herself. She'd even looked, but couldn't find anything. Her father had hidden his crimes well over the years. But not well enough since he had been given a life sentence.

He'd died in prison that first year. She'd heard about his death but, after talking with her sister, they hadn't attended his funeral. The two of them had visited their mother's grave that same day, holding hands and letting the tears flow, but neither had understood those tears.

Shaking her mind out of the past, she walked over to her desk and typed in Drake's name. She'd followed his career over the past six years, but there were always new articles to read. Obviously, she wasn't the only one that was fascinated by the man! The press loved him, followed him around and reported on not only his business successes but also his personal life, whenever they caught even the smallest rumor.

A split second after she pressed enter on her computer, she saw a long list of articles about the man. Irritated that she was distracted, she read through the first few articles. And then one more, and one more. He actually had created one of the largest construction companies in the country with his headquarters based out of Chicago. So what was he doing here in Denver? And why would his holding company, which had huge assets globally, be interested in a mid-sized architectural firm? She'd always assumed that Harrison Holdings would have a team of architects on staff. They didn't just build houses or even large buildings. Harrison Holdings was known for building cities!

With a sigh, she clicked out of her web search, refusing to read anything more about the man's career or his astounding wealth. So what if he lived in a fabulous house that was perched on the top of a mountain in what looked like a visually precarious design? She'd glanced at the designs and she'd done similar work on her own dream house. She absolutely loved designing homes, creating either small or large living environments for the way each family lived. Designing buildings and sports complexes was interesting also, but her favorite projects were those where she got to sit down and talk with a family, find out what they did each day or during the year so she could create the perfect area for each member of the family.

Shaking her head, she focused all of her attention on the building she was currently working on, pushing aside the possible motives of a mega-billionaire with dark, piercing eyes and shoulders that were....she closed her eyes and pursed her lips, irritated with herself for even picturing the man's shoulders. At least it was just his shoulders, she told herself. She hadn't gone down the road of picturing the man...Ugh!

Okay, so he probably looked amazing without that dark, tailored suit covering his tall, muscular body. That was no reason to break her concentration and picture the man naked. She had an important meeting in only a few minutes and she needed to get some last minute details into the design.

CHAPTER 2

Unfortunately, her meeting time arrived and she was still unable to focus on the issues so she had to speak to her ideas instead of having them incorporated into the design. Another mark against Drake Harrison, since he was the reason why she hadn't been able to focus on her work. She could blame herself, especially after her gluttonous reading on the man's career and the tidbits of personal life the media had been able to dig up, but she'd never had this issue before.

After the meeting, she stomped into her office, slapping down her papers and still irritated with Drake for his interruption this morning.

She never had this problem! In fact, most people teased her that she focused too much!

"Are you coming to the luncheon?" Dave Anderson asked, poking his head into Sierra's office.

Dave was a very sweet guy who had been consistently inviting her to the weekly happy hours at the bar around the corner from their office. Sierra hadn't wanted to encourage his interest, so she'd declined all of the invitations so far although she went out to lunches with some of her co-workers. She didn't want to be antisocial but she didn't want to encourage Dave when she felt nothing more than friendship for the man.

"I just had a difficult meeting," she said, rubbing her forehead. "I'm going to pass on the lunch. Can you cover for me?" she asked, feeling slightly guilty for asking him to do something like that.

"Sure can," he replied, eager to finally have a task from her.

Sierra almost groaned at his enthusiasm. It wasn't like she was asking him to kill a dragon or anything, but Dave hadn't been subtle about his interest in her. Had she just given him unintended encouragement?

She slumped down into her desk chair, feeling like a horrible person. How could she kill off the man's interest? He was a sweet guy, but she just wasn't interested.

She almost groaned as she squeezed her frustration ball with her left hand while her pencil sketched out the details of her next idea with her right. She wasn't aware of the ball's eyes bugging out. All of her attention was on trying to figure out her next move. How could she keep Drake Harrison away from her, keep him from discovering who she was? She simply couldn't let him connect her to her father!

Biting her pencil, she stood back and surveyed the work she'd done on her drawing board. She bit her lip slightly and surveyed the changes she'd incorporated so far and smiled with satisfaction. She bent over the table, grateful for her ability to focus only on work, kick out all the other details that made her uncomfortable. Life was suddenly too complicated, she thought as the words to Miranda Lambert's "Mamma's Broken Heart" spinning through her mind.

Hours later, Drake looked around at the empty offices, his eyes alert to anyone who might still be working at this hour. It was Thursday night and he knew that most of the staff had left to head to the local bar for drinks and to gossip about the news of his takeover. He understood their anxiety and had tried to limit their worries over lunch today, but he knew that there would always be some people in an office environment that would perceive the worst in any kind of change. They were usually the less talented workers, trying to find justification for their lack of accomplishments by gossiping about the others who were more dedicated.

He wasn't overly concerned about those people, thinking that he and his transition team had done a good job of minimizing the anxiety over lunch today.

But now it was after hours and he was intent on trapping his fly-away butterfly. Sierra Colbert had avoided him all afternoon but now, he was going to get to know her a bit better.

"You're here late," a deep voice said from behind her.

Sierra jumped out of her chair and spun around. When she saw the tall, awe inspiring man leaning against her doorway, she gasped and almost fell sideways.

Trying to regain her composure as quickly as possible, she stepped to the side, while at the same time, hiding the papers she'd been working on.

Unfortunately, her composure wasn't having such a good day and she started to slide over, her feet not properly braced far enough apart.

With a swift move, Drake moved forward, catching Sierra before she could fall on her face to the floor.

With his hands wrapped around her, she couldn't help but grab his arms, her hands wrapping around surprisingly large biceps hidden by the relatively tame-looking dark suit.

Slowly, and with great reluctance, she looked up at him, her entire body tingling with awareness of this moment. Her body was plastered against his, even his right leg was pressed between her legs, pushing her skirt up higher on her thighs. A part of her wanted to die of humiliation but a larger part of her wanted to press her hands against his arms, to slide them higher, testing for other muscles. Perhaps if she could slide her fingers over, feel his chest…

"I'm sorry," she gasped, suddenly realizing what she was doing and pulled herself out of his embrace, her face flaming with color at both her thoughts as well as her clumsiness. She wasn't usually like that but he'd surprised her and she really didn't like surprises. "Thank you for your assistance." Her voice had dropped to a whisper now and she tried to step backwards, but the table was behind her and his huge body was blocking everything in front of her.

"My pleasure," he commented, his voice deep and husky.

They stood like that for a long, pregnant moment, both of them staring, neither moving. Sierra tried to breathe, but his touch was making that impossible. She wanted so desperately to feel him, to examine those muscles underneath the deceptive suit, to find out what it would be like if he were to kiss her…

Drake's mind was reeling with how incredibly soft she was. His hands were still holding her waist and his leg could feel the muscles in her own. He wanted to lean forward, to feel her breasts against his chest again and taste those pink lips, to find out what she tasted like.

And she smelled terrific. Something in his brain caught her perfume and he knew he'd smelled that scent before, but he couldn't place it. Rose? No, not that. But something flowery. Something fresh and alive. Something that made him think of….

He couldn't place it, but it there was something so familiar about that scent. "Where are you from?" he asked his voice husky and deeper than normal. He watched her face but wouldn't give her enough room to feel comfortable. He knew he should step backwards, but there was just something about the way that she smelled that kept him close, made him want to move closer and eliminate all barriers between them, both physical and psychological.

Damn, he loved a mystery!

Sierra was instantly wary, not wanting to let him connect her past with his. She couldn't tell him that she'd grown up in Chicago, knowing that his company was headquartered there. He would ask too many questions and she most likely couldn't answer any of them without giving him more clues to her past. And more specifically, clues to the connection they shared. "I live over off of Golden Road."

He immediately was aware that she'd told him where she currently lived and not where she used to live. So she didn't want him to know about her past?

Interesting. It only added to the puzzle that was quickly growing around this lovely woman.

He could tell by the stubborn jut of her chin that she wouldn't reveal anything else at the moment. He almost smiled with anticipation. This woman would be his, he thought with a determination he hadn't felt in a long, long time. In fact, he hadn't felt this strongly about a woman since he'd left the hospital six years ago, determined to find the mystery woman who had sat beside him almost constantly. She'd disappeared when he'd regained consciousness and he hadn't been able to find a trace of her.

Interesting that they were both brunettes, he thought. Regardless, he wanted this woman with an intense desire and he was confident that feeling was reciprocated. He just had to understand why she was resisting the attraction.

"Are you ready to go?" he asked, shifting slightly so that she was standing on her own. Not by choice. If it were up to him, he would have pushed her back, pressing her up onto her desk and then he could bend down and kiss her neck, smell that perfume again.

Instead, he stepped backwards and gave her space. She quickly stepped away from him, putting a chair between the two of them.

"Go?" she asked, her eyes wide with confusion while she gripped the back of the chair. "I wasn't planning to go anywhere."

"We're going out to dinner," he said firmly. He chuckled when she pulled her head back as if she thought he was crazy. "You don't read your e-mail messages very often, do you?"

She ignored his question that seemed irrelevant. "Why would I be going out to dinner with you?"

One side of his mouth went up but he once again suppressed his amusement. "The message stated that anyone who had missed the lunch because they were too busy would have an opportunity to talk with me during dinner and get out any questions they might have."

She reared back in horror. "What? No! I don't...that is, I didn't mean..." Boy had her plan to avoid him backfired!

He reached up and pushed a stray lock of hair behind her ear. "You didn't mean to have any sort of association with me. Is that what you're trying to say?"

"Yes!" she almost sighed with relief that he completely understood and didn't seem to be offended. And then she realized what she'd just admitted to and shook her head. "No. I'm sorry, that came out wrong. I didn't mean to say that..."

He moved closer, his eyes gentle as he looked down into her anxious, blue eyes. "You didn't mean to admit that the attraction between the two of us is so strong that you're having trouble focusing?"

She blinked and started to shake her head. How could he know that? "No. That isn't what I was going to say." And it wasn't. She'd never admit that to him. Good grief, she wouldn't even admit it to herself!

"You were going to tell me that you're sorry that you missed the lunch today? And that you have many questions about how the firm is going to move forward with new management, right?" He took her hand in his, causing her body to begin that embarrassing trembling once again.

He was already leading her out the door, handing her the purse that she'd just dumped beside her desk earlier that day. With his hand on the small of her back and his towering height, she was too flustered to rally her senses and stop their forward momentum.

She took her purse, holding it in front of her as if it were some sort of shield that could ward off the impact his closeness had on her. She shook her head, denying what was actually happening. "But I don't want to go to dinner with you."

He didn't laugh at her outburst but continued to walk her out of her office and down the hallway. "Of course you don't."

She didn't get the sense that he was going to let her out of it though. "Mr. Harrison, I really don't…"

Drake pressed the button for the elevator and turned back to face her. "You have several projects that are ongoing at the moment and you don't have time, even though you put in more hours than anyone else in the firm. So I understand your reticence to take any time off, but I'm going to have to insist in this situation." He couldn't resist touching her arm when the janitorial staff pushed their carts down behind her. She wasn't aware of their approach but it gave him another chance to touch her, even if it was only her slender arm as he shifted their stance so the large, heavy carts could pass by them. "But you're going to be on a very big project next week. So you really need to understand the ins and outs of what's happening, all the changes that will be occurring." Tonight would have nothing to do with explaining his management, the changes or even the project he planned to put her on next week. It was only about the two of them getting to know each other better. But if he told her that, she would run away, scared out of her mind.

The doors to the elevator closed and she blinked, wishing she could think more quickly. Normally, she was able to put a man in his place easily, usually with just a simple look that said, "Don't even bother." If words were needed to discourage a man, she was quick witted and cutting, showing her displeasure at any man who invaded her personal space.

In this case, this man wasn't hearing her well placed put-downs because, unfortunately, he didn't give her a chance to come up with one. He was just moving forward as if she had completely agreed to his plans.

When they were standing beside a very powerful, very elegant looking black sedan, he opened the door for her but she finally got her wits about her. "Mr. Harrison…"

He interrupted her and shifted slightly, their new positions more intimate somehow since his broad shoulders and impressive height blocked out the overhead lights in the parking garage. "Call me Drake. And I'll call you Sierra."

He was standing too close, she thought. She had to tilt her head way back just to look into his eyes and that didn't help her convey the look that would have him back off. "I don't want to call you anything," she said, but her voice sounded more breathless than she'd wanted. She was going for firm, commanding and intimidating. Why was it coming out as if she was wondering what it would be like to be kissed by those firm, sexy lips?

She shook her head. "I really need to…"

"Get in the car, Sierra."

She blinked once again. The look in his eyes was telling her that he wasn't going to ask again. She thought about arguing, of just taking her keys out of her purse and walking directly to her own car, ignoring the commanding tone in his voice and leaving him here.

But something in his eyes dared her, challenged her. Was he daring her to walk away? Or to get into the car? She wasn't sure what it was, and even if she could define it, she wasn't sure if she could dismiss it. The heat emanating from his body warmed her, the warmth radiating out from her stomach and spreading outwards, creating an excitement that she didn't quite understand.

"What if I don't?" she questioned, not sure if she really had the confidence to challenge him.

He moved closer, his body almost pressing her against the car. "If you don't want to get in the car, I can only assume you want to kiss me as much as I want to kiss you. We're standing here, no one else is around, why not give in to what we both want? I'm going to kiss by the end of the evening anyway so you've now been forewarned, Sierra."

A part of her, a very large part of her mind and her body, wanted him to bend down low and follow through on that threat. But the smaller, more sensible, part of her mind, the part that seemed to have at least a modicum of sense still functioning, didn't have the courage to call his bluff. Because she didn't think he was bluffing. The look in those blue eyes told her that he wanted her to dare him, wanted her to keep on standing there against his car so he could kiss her.

She was already sitting in the plush leather seats by the time she realized what she was doing. She watched with fascination as he walked around the front of the car, his long, muscular legs taking him around quickly. Before she had time to take a breath, or more specifically, before her mind realized that she had a small break from him, he was sliding into the seat next to her. She watched with interest as he folded his long, incredible length into the leather seat beside her. His body seemed to take up all the available space but that was crazy since the car more than accommodated his long legs and deliciously broad shoulders.

She tore her eyes away from his muscular thigh, staring out into the darkness in front of her. "You said that all the others who missed the lunch would also be attending. Why aren't you driving them to wherever we're going?"

She almost gasped when he put his arm around the back of her seat, leaning forward slightly. She thought he was about to make a move on her and her heartbeat went into overdrive. But he was only shifting slightly so he could see out the rear view window.

But as soon as he was turned slightly, making his broad shoulders almost come into contact with hers and invading her personal space once again, he said, "You're the only one who missed the lunch. The others were all eager to meet me, to talk to me about their expertise and explain why they were essential to the firm's success."

Her mouth dropped open slightly. She knew it wasn't because of his words or the surprise at his cynicism at her co-worker's eagerness to maintain their jobs. It was simply because he was so close, his heat almost a physical force in the confines of the luxurious car.

He drove the powerful car with confidence, almost arrogance as he asked her questions about her current projects. As she answered his questions, relieved that they were work-related, she realized that she never felt unsure of his driving abilities as he easily moved between the slower traffic. When he pulled into an underground parking garage, she was relieved to be able to step out of the vehicle and breathe in air that wasn't saturated with his spicy, male scent.

Unfortunately, he came around the car too quickly for her. She hadn't had time to clear her mind, refuel her thoughts and get her equilibrium back in balance. Then his hand touched the small of her back again and she almost resented how quickly he could make her feel protected and secure. Which was a contradiction actually since the man made her quiver with strange feelings that she didn't think she liked. So how could she feel safe and secure while at the same time, worried and....trembly? Was that even a word? Her mind really had turned to mush.

"What's the name of the restaurant?" she asked as they both stepped into the elevator. Something deep in her stomach tightened when she noticed him put a key into the control panel and pressed a button.

"I'm cooking for you," he said as he pulled the key out and let it slip into the pocket of his slacks. "I hope you like Italian."

Sierra swallowed past the lump in her throat and unconsciously moved to the back corner of the elevator. Leaning against the rich paneling, she stared up at the numbers indicating that the elevator was quickly ascending. All the way to the top.

"You live in the penthouse," she stated. A split second later, the elevator doors opened and she gasped in surprise at the beauty in front of her. She forgot her fears as she stepped out, walking slowly towards the floor to ceiling windows that showed the most magnificent view of the Rocky Mountains she'd ever seen in her life. "This is incredible," she sighed with awe.

"Thanks. It certainly is relaxing. And a huge change from my place in Chicago." He moved away slightly but Sierra couldn't pull her eyes away from the view. "Would you like a glass of wine?" he asked almost softly so as not to disturb her.

"That would be lovely," she said, and finally looked away. What she saw when she looked at his apartment, and the man, was almost as amazing. This penthouse was like an actual home with interesting details, quirky pendant lights hanging over the countertops, extremely comfortable looking bar stools with deep cushions instead of those uncomfortable wooden ones most people preferred because of their sleek lines, not because anyone actually wanted to sit on them. There was strategic lighting and a massive granite fireplace that switched on, warming up the whole area.

She found Drake behind the counter, uncorking a bottle of red wine, and then pouring the rich liquid into two round goblets. He handed one to her and she was almost afraid to reach out and take it, afraid her hands were shaking too much to hold the delicate looking crystal.

She accepted the crystal goblet warily, careful not to touch his hands during the transfer.

"To new beginnings," he said and raised his glass towards her before taking a sip.

Sierra didn't want to drink to new beginnings or old endings or any kind of change. Change was for her clients. She worked change around their lives and their preferences. Personally, she didn't like change. Change meant something unexpected, something different. It was hard to anticipate how to react to something new and different. Change could be good, but why risk it?

She'd gone through enough change in her life. She liked the dull, predictable life she'd built for herself. And this man was here to stir things up, impact her world and shake things so she might not even recognize her life.

"What are you thinking?" he asked as he pulled his tie loose, and then tossed it onto the counter away from the food he'd pulled out of the refrigerator.

She took a long sip of wine, just as an excuse to give her more time to come up with an answer. "I was wondering who decorated your space. It's very...eclectic." She wasn't about to tell him that she didn't want anything in her life to change and that she resented him for bringing it all here. She resented him even more for making her feel things that she didn't like and she thought she could actually learn to hate the man for being so gorgeous and healthy. And close! They weren't ever supposed to meet so why was he here now? Why had fate stepped in and made this whole day so...awkward!

Drake looked around, nodding his head at her description. "I decorated it myself. I've been in this industry long enough to know what I like and don't like."

That surprised her enough to distract herself from her mutinous thoughts and she looked around at the lights and the comfortable seating area which would allow his guests to relax while he cooked, but still be near the fireplace. "Really? That's surprising," she said without thinking.

"Why is that so strange?" he asked, setting his glass down on the granite counters so he could fill up a pot with water for the pasta.

"I just can't picture you as the decorator type."

He smiled at her observation. "Well, I guess I cheat a little. When I build a hotel or apartment complex, the designers do all the work. If I like a particular item or set of pieces, I have those pieces shipped to a storage facility. Since I change living spaces frequently, I just choose the pieces I want for any particular apartment I've bought. So I guess I don't really stroll through the furniture warehouses to find the perfect sofa or chair like so many designers or couples do when trying to decorate their new space."

She looked around at the lighting that perfectly suited the seating arrangements, the angles of the fireplace that were just slightly off center so the kitchen looked balanced. This is the type of thing she loved doing, but he'd done it all himself. "It's a unique style," she said softly, feeling vaguely threatened. If she were to design a living space, she'd do it exactly like this.

Deciding that a change in topics was needed, she walked around, acting as if she were looking at things when in reality, she was painfully aware of him cooking, chopping and seasoning whatever it was that he was making. "So why did you buy Todd's firm? Don't you have a whole team of architects on staff?"

"Of course."

"So why did you need us?"

"Because your team knows this area better than mine. You're very successful with the clients and understand the cultural issues that come with entering any new market. Each area of the country is different with fads and preferences that are unique to the region."

She had to accept that his explanation made sense. It still didn't explain why he chose Todd's company though. "So why did you approach Todd to buy out his firm?" She sat down on one of the comfortable stools, propping her chin up on the palm of her hand so she could watch him. A fascinating show, she thought.

He placed a plate of crackers with some sort of dip in a small bowl in front of her. "What would you say if I told you that I bought out Todd because I wanted you on the team?"

She immediately rolled her eyes. "Seriously, what was it about Todd's group that made you choose them over all the other architectural firms in the city?"

Drake watched with interest as she sampled the creamy pesto dip, gratified when her eyebrows went up in surprise. Since she didn't believe that her reputation preceded her, he would go with a more simplistic approach. "The talent in Todd's group is better, he's ready to retire and I wanted to move ahead quickly. Other firms might not be as amenable to a fast-paced change, but since Todd was already past retirement age, everyone on your team seemed to be anticipating someone else taking over."

"You realize the person we all expected to take over was Mark Peterson, right?"

Drake nodded. "I've already tagged him as a problem issue."

She was curious, "What are you going to do to neutralize him?" As soon as she said that, she realized what she'd said and how it might come across. More specifically, how it could remind him of that painful period in his past. Her father had repeatedly used the term neutralize when there was a threat. "Neutralize" in organized crime lingo meant "get rid of the guy – permanently".

"Do you always talk about work in order to avoid personal problems?" he asked, more curious than ever. She was sitting on the bar stool looking like she was ready to bolt and the only thing keeping her in place was his cooking. She was pretty cute when she peered over the counter to try and see what he was slicing up. She'd never figure it out since it was all going into a pan. But he enjoyed her attempts since, whenever she leaned forward, her silk blouse fell open slightly and he could see the soft, perfect swells of her breasts. Once he even spied the lace of her bra.

"I thought this whole dinner thing was about me asking questions about work." She hid her face behind her glass as she took another sip of her wine.

He chuckled and tossed in some crushed garlic. "No you didn't. You know exactly what this dinner is about and it has nothing to do with work."

Her hand halted halfway to her mouth, the cracker and dip completely forgotten as she watched him, his eyes heating up with anticipation. "I came here because…"

Drake spread his arms out, bracing them on the countertop as he looked into her eyes, not letting her mis-read the message he was trying to convey. "Because we're both attracted to each other and you wanted to get to know me better."

She shook her head, but something in her stomach tightened in a very exciting way, a trembling began that she didn't completely understand. "I don't…"

"Stop right there, Sierra," he said firmly, turning the knife so it was laying safely on the wooden cutting board. "You need to be completely honest here. I can see you trembling and I know that you're just as affected as I am by our closeness."

"No…" she started to say, only to have him shake his head.

"I understand that something is holding you back from enjoying the fire that's quickly burning us both up. So I'll give you space until you give me an indication that you're ready. But until then, don't even try to deny this thing between us. I won't buy it."

He picked up his knife again and finished off the red peppers he'd been dicing.

Sierra swallowed, unsure how to respond. She wanted desperately to just run away but there wasn't anywhere to hide.

He didn't let her talk about work any longer. He asked her questions about her personal life, about her school and why she'd chosen to become an architect. The pasta was finished and he drained it all in the sink, and then turned off the heat underneath the sauce. "This looks done," he finally said, smiling because she kept nibbling at the crackers and dip. He carried two plates filled with pasta and a rich, creamy tomato sauce over to the table near the fireplace. "Can you bring the wine?" he asked, putting her plate on the table.

All through dinner, he had her laughing at his antics as he grew up and they both shared hilarious stories about different requests clients had made over the years. Sierra relaxed for the first time that night, feeling wonderful with the amazing food and the delicious wine, not to mention his dark, sexy eyes laughing with her. It also helped that he was across the table from her. The solid wood gave her a slight sense of security from his unrelenting sexual appeal that she was finding very difficult to ignore.

"Dinner was delicious," she said, picking up her plate so she could bring it to the kitchen.

"Don't worry about that," he said, taking the plate away from her. "My housekeeper will come in tomorrow morning and clean everything up."

Sierra didn't like that one little bit. Because that meant she didn't have anything to do with her hands, no barrier to keep him at bay. "It's no problem," she countered and picked up his plate and wine glass. "You cooked. I don't mind doing the dishes. Besides, leaving them overnight will make the food dry out." She didn't look at him as she set the plate down in the sink and turned on the faucet.

"Sierra," his deep voice said from right behind her. He reached around, placing the dish he'd just taken away from her under the water. He then easily shut off the water. Turning her around, he watched with both amusement and sexual frustration as she stood stiffly in the loose circle of his arms. "Why are you so afraid of me?" he asked gently.

Sierra wanted to fold her hands together, to close him out but she couldn't drop her hands because they would be too close to sensitive areas of his anatomy. She crossed them over her chest, not daring to look up at him. "I'm not afraid of you," she lied. "I just don't really like you."

He laughed softly and Sierra was impressed with his self-confidence. "You're lying again. I don't understand why, but I'm going to find out." He kissed her neck, her earlobe. "I'm going to discover all of your secrets."

She shivered with his touch, actually leaning her head to the side to give him better access. But then she realized what she was doing, what he'd just said, and she stepped around him, relieved when he let her put some space between their bodies. "I don't have any secrets," she lied again although her words came out sounding breathless and too shaky.

He watched her with amusement as she walked over to her purse, putting it over her shoulder in a silent command that she was now leaving. "Everyone has secrets," he countered. "One of yours is why you're so afraid of me."

She almost rolled her eyes, more confident now that she wasn't in his arms and he wasn't kissing her like he had been moments ago. "You flatter yourself. I'm not afraid of you. I'm just not interested."

One of his dark eyebrows went up with her flagrant challenge. "So you're saying that, if I were to go over to you and kiss you, you wouldn't respond?"

With a firm grip on the strap of her purse, she shook her head. She couldn't pull her eyes away from his mouth though. Her mind instantly imagined what it would be like if he were to kiss her, wondering if he was gentle or rough, demanding. Her eyes traveled lower, taking in his broad shoulders and the biceps that pushed against his dress shirt that was now open at his throat, revealing the dark hair that her fingers ached to touch, to run through and test its texture.

"No," she gritted out, not realizing that her body had softened, that he'd seen the way her eyes had traveled down his body and he'd even noticed her nipples that were now pushing against the silk material of her blouse. "No," she repeated, more for herself than anything else, "I wouldn't like that at all."

He walked over to her, looking down into her eyes. "You can't hide it forever, Sierra."

She stiffened at his bold statement. "I don't have anything to hide."

His finger reached out and touched the pulse throbbing at the base of her throat. She almost snapped at him when one of those dark eyebrows went up once again. "And I really hate it when you do that." She spun around on her heel, walking purposefully towards the elevator. "I'll catch a cab home. Thank you very much for dinner and for taking the time to answer all of my questions."

Drake walked behind her, enjoying the view as she walked swiftly away from him. He grabbed his keys from the table where he'd tossed them when they'd first arrived, following her into the elevator.

She looked up at him, startled by his presence in the small confines of the elevator's cab. "What are you doing?" she demanded, moving away, putting as much space between them as possible although it wasn't much. It might be a relatively big elevator, but he was a relatively huge man and just his shoulders took up a lot of space. She wasn't used to men ignoring her statements and it irritated her that he was the first.

"I'm going to drive you home."

He said that as if it were obvious, as if she hadn't just told him that she would take a cab home. Her anger welled up to almost choke her. "You know, I much preferred you when…" she started to say that she preferred him when he was in a hospital bed not giving out orders to her but stopped herself just in time.

He was instantly alert, his sharp eyes taking in the quick blush that stained her beautiful skin. "You much preferred me when…?" he prompted. His eyes narrowed as he looked down into her startled expression. "Have we met before?"

She shook her head and lowered her eyes. Taking the offensive, she turned to face the doors. "I hope that I'm not that unmemorable. If we'd met before, perhaps you were too drunk to remember me." She knew it was a lame comeback, especially since he'd only had one glass of wine the whole time they'd been having dinner. Even while he was cooking, he was very careful. Darn it! Another mark in his favor!

She couldn't let him see her eyes though. The lie of omission still made her feel guilty. Her father had lied all the time, kept secrets from everyone. She didn't want to be like him and struggled to keep her silence. It was all for the greater good, she told herself.

Is that what her father had told himself, she wondered? Had he justified his cruelty by saying that he was providing someone a job? Or he was making a home for his children?

No! Her father had been a self-centered bastard. She might not have done enough, or anything, to take him down, but she wasn't like him. She wasn't dishonest or cruel. She was keeping her identity from Drake only to keep him from remembering a horrible time in his life.

Well, and to make sure he didn't fire her.

She sighed. That was where she was selfish, she thought with resignation. She was protecting herself from his memories and retribution.

Another mark in his favor, she thought. She looked at him out of the corner of her eye as they descended in the elevator. She didn't know for sure, but Drake didn't seem like the kind of man who would shy away from the truth.

He might not ever be able to be her fantasy man, but after knowing a conscious Drake Harrison for only one day, he was definitely starting to have several good points in his favor.

Not that she was counting them up or anything. Besides, he had several bad points as well.

The elevator doors opened up at that moment and she gritted her teeth when she realized that he had taken them down to the garage level. If she'd been more on her game instead of letting him taunt her, she would have noticed that he'd pressed the garage button instead of the lobby button. She could have gotten a cab if she'd thought to press the lobby instead of the garage. Now she'd have to argue with him to go back up, a losing proposition she suspected, or allow him to drive her home.

And it would figure that the man would have the closest parking space! "I really don't want to put you out," she said, taking a deep breath. "Those are the stairs to the lobby. I'll just call a cab from there and will head home." She took two steps in that direction, her whole body tense to see if he would allow her the freedom to get home on her own.

Obviously, she should have known better. Her day simply wasn't turning out very well.

He took hold of her upper arm and steered her right back in the direction of his car. Within moments, she was sitting in the seat and watching him walk around. She shook her head with embarrassment and frustration when she realized that she was staring at his ever-so-nice butt. Couldn't she just leave the poor guy alone? And couldn't he leave her alone?

She wondered what it would be like if she'd met him for the first time today. Would she be just as irritated by his demeanor? Would she become angered by his arrogance?

Yes, she thought as he slipped into the car beside her. There was just something about this man that irked her. She didn't like the way she felt all quivery and hot when he got close to her and that had nothing to do with her fear of him realizing that her father was the man who had ordered his death.

The man just wasn't her type, she thought as she stared out the window while he backed out of the parking space.

They drove in silence for several minutes before Sierra realized that he was heading for Washington Park. She lived in Washington Park! "How do you know where I live?" she asked, straightening in her seat.

He glanced over at her quickly. "I find you fascinating, Sierra. So I read your personnel file." With a lascivious leer he said, "When you decide that you're finished running away from me, I can be at your house in less than ten minutes." He laughed softly, the deep, grumbling sound made her heart flutter with awareness. "And you told me where you lived earlier today."

She hated the heat that flushed through her with his assurance. She didn't like him, she got irritated with everything he said and she definitely didn't want him rushing over to her place. "I don't know what is so interesting about me. I'm just an ordinary female." She turned to stare back out of the windshield. "I put my slacks on the same way everyone else does in the morning."

She could actually feel his smile without turning to look at him. "I don't believe you. Let me watch you put your slacks on tomorrow morning," he said with another one of those sexy laughs.

She wished she was one of those people who had a pithy comeback for whatever was said. But she was more math oriented, and the humor bone had been left out when God made her. So she sat in the ultra-luxurious seat, fuming at his wit. She sighed with relief when he turned down the street where her apartment was. "I don't think I like just anyone being able to read my personnel file. Those records are for management. They're supposed to be private."

He chuckled as he turned into her parking lot. "I think you're forgetting that I'm now your management."

She gritted her teeth to keep herself from responding. "Thank you again for dinner," she said when he turned the corner into her parking lot.

He pulled into a parking space near her building and turned off the engine. When she started to reach for the door handle, he stopped her with his strong hand on her forearm. She turned back to him, wanting to just jump out of the car, but something in his tone stopped her, made her listen. "Sierra, just a head's up that you'll be working on a special project starting tomorrow."

That captured her attention and her hand on the door froze. "What kind of special project?" She was both wary and alert, trying to read the truth in his eyes through the darkness. She shook her head suddenly. "It doesn't matter. I have too many projects right now. I mentioned this earlier today. I can't take on anything else." She remembered her manners and forced a smile. "Thank you for the opportunity though," she said, even though she had no idea what the opportunity was.

He ignored her rejection of the new project and continued on as if she hadn't said anything at all. "Come to Todd's office tomorrow morning at nine. Everything will be explained to you."

She sighed with relief. Todd's office was safe. She didn't need to be wary of having to speak with this man tomorrow. "I'll be there. Thank you."

As she quickly left his car, completely aware that he was watching her while she walked into her building, Sierra wondered what the special project might be. But she resisted the urge to turn around and ask him. She didn't want to give him any encouragement. The man was confident enough as it was and she'd just told him unequivocally that she wouldn't have the bandwidth to take on any new projects at this point.

She didn't sleep well that night, her mind going over the conversation with Drake during dinner, wondering how she could have gotten so wrapped up in both the laughter as well as the ever increasing sexual tension and had such a nice evening. Well, except for the moments when he was being irritating, that is. And the times when he'd kissed her. She definitely hadn't enjoyed those moments.

She punched her pillow and glared out the darkened window. She was lying again. It was one thing to lie to him because she told herself she was protecting him. But even that was a lie. She was protecting herself. She was protecting her job.

She sighed, feeling sad all of a sudden. She didn't know what to do or how to deal with this man. For the first time in a very long time, her future was unclear in her mind.

CHAPTER 3

She tossed and turned that night, staring at the ceiling for hours until she finally went into her kitchen to get a cup of warm milk. That put her to sleep, but because she was so exhausted from a rough night, she didn't wake up with enough time to get ready.

There was a text on her cell phone from the very man that had invaded her dreams last night, informing her that he'd arranged to have her car delivered to her apartment. And even at such a thoughtful gesture, she refused to give him points for being considerate. If he hadn't forced her to dinner, she wouldn't have left her car at the office.

Good grief, she thought s she pushed herself to move faster. She was even being petty now!

Mentally reviewing her schedule while she jumped into the shower, she knew that she didn't have any clients today, nor any meetings that would put her in the hallways too often. So instead of the normal, stiff business suit she wore to the office, she pulled out a pair of black slacks and a soft, pink sweater. It was much more comfortable and, hopefully, she could get more work done today. She didn't even bother to pull her hair back, just blow drying it straight and letting it hang over her shoulders and down her back. It felt good to be so free and she chose flowery shoes that would match her pink sweater. Feeling pretty and courageous, she grabbed her purse and headed out into the day. She was pretty sure she wouldn't run into one outrageous, gorgeous and sexually enticing male, but if she did, she felt better prepared today.

As she drove into the office, only a little later than normal, her mind went over different ways she could avoid Drake if he actually showed up in the office. She doubted he would be there. She knew that the man had massive construction projects all over the world. So he definitely didn't have the time to schmooze with all the little people two days in a row.

It worried her that the acquisition might force them all to move to a different city. She loved the Denver area and would fight to stay here if that was possible. But if it was a non-starter, if Harrison Holdings was going to move everyone to their headquarters in Chicago, she would just resign and find another job. She definitely couldn't move back to Chicago. Too many people knew who she was and she didn't want any connection to her old life. She'd created a new one and she much preferred this one to the life her father had created around his criminal enterprises.

Maybe she could go out on her own. If Drake wanted to move everyone to Chicago, would she have the courage to start her own architectural design firm here in Denver? The thought was enticing but could she afford it? What would she really need to get started? Besides clients, that is. A website, definitely. But her sister Marissa was a genius at that. So no problems there. What else would be needed besides office furniture and an advertising budget? She wasn't exactly sure what she had in her bank account, but surely it wouldn't require too much up front money to get started. And if it kept her away from one gorgeous, dangerous male that scared the heejeebees out of her, wasn't it worth it?

She was lost in thought as she walked into the office, smiling absently at Belinda, the receptionist, who always had a bright, happy smile for everyone that came through the doors.

When she reached her office, she saw the note attached to the middle of her current work project. It was written in a bold scrawl and just reminded her of the nine o'clock appointment with Todd. Something inside of her started to get that funny feeling again as she read and re-read the words on the note. No matter how many times she tried to rationalize the message, she knew with certainty that it had been personally written and placed here by Drake.

He was getting around her forgetfulness about reading her e-mail messages. Drat the man! Why was he always one step ahead of her?

She glanced at her watch as she stored her purse in her desk drawer. Glancing at her watch, she knew she didn't have much time because of her sleepless night and her late arrival. So instead of sitting down and going through her projects one more time, she crumpled the note, tossed it in the recycling bin and grabbed her notebook so she could head down the hallway towards Todd's office. She would get there a bit earlier than needed, but she knew she wouldn't be able to concentrate on something for a short period of time, knowing she'd have to stop in only a few minutes.

She stood outside the closed door, leaning her head against the wood and mentally bracing herself for a confrontation with Drake. What outrageous thing would he suggest today? Would he...she simply didn't know what that man would do. She thought about him in the hospital bed six years ago, holding his hand and watching his chest, willing him to breathe, praying almost non-stop that he would survive and recover well enough to have a good life. It meant that her father hadn't won, at least in this instance.

If her father were still alive, he would be furious to learn that the man was even more buff now than he was back then. Why had her father even beaten Drake? What had been the reason? Of course, her father was so horrible, he might not have a reason for his brutality, but she hoped that he had some sort of reasoning and it hadn't just been for amusement.

"Any chance you might share?"

Sierra jumped, spinning around and almost tripping over her own feet. Drake reached out and easily steadied her before she made a fool of herself and Sierra vehemently wished she didn't react this way whenever he was around. This was the third time he'd surprised her and she was really becoming irritated with the problem. Why was she so jumpy? What was it about his deep, gravelly voice that just...did something to her?

"Why do you have to sneak up on me like that?" she growled angrily, trying to move out of his arms but he held her still as he looked down into her angry, blue eyes.

"What were you smiling about?" he asked, standing very close, his hands still on her waist and his large hands conveying his heat even through her pink sweater.

She looked confused with his sudden closeness. She'd been mentally girding herself to see him so his sudden presence and his intimate closeness surprised her. Even the way his body was so large caused her breath to catch in her throat. His height and the breadth of his shoulders blocked out almost all the light as well as the other people who might be passing by. It was as if they were in their own world, completely private and sensuously intimate.

"I wasn't really smiling," she whispered. She cleared her throat. "I have that meeting you reminded me about."

He smiled slightly, his eyes dropping down to her lips. "See? I'm already starting to learn your secrets."

She blinked, confused by his statement. "What secret?" her heart panicked. Please don't let him make the connection! It suddenly occurred to her that, maybe if Drake knew who her father was, he would be so repulsed he would leave her alone. Then these confusing feelings that continued to swamp her every time she was near him would go away and she could get on with her life. He wouldn't want to touch her if he knew who her father was.

He looked at her with concern and curiosity. "Why does the idea of me discovering your secrets terrify you so much?" he asked softly, his long finger sliding gently down her cheek. "You're not a criminal, are you?" he asked with a teasing grin.

She grabbed his finger, her whole body shaking at how close he'd come. It didn't matter that they'd known each other for less than twenty-four hours. The man was already closer to her, impacted her senses more than any other man she'd ever dated. She was twenty-four years old and had never been near a man who could make her feel anything so intensely as this man.

Oh why couldn't it have been someone else? Someone she didn't fear! Someone who wouldn't hate her when he learned the truth of her past.

She blinked and stepped to the side. Why was she even thinking that? She didn't like this man! He was arrogant and irritating. And he always invaded her space, making her feel small and...delicate! She wasn't ever delicate! She was strong and capable. She'd had to be in order to survive in her father's household. She and her sister were tough! Definitely not delicate.

"You never know if I'm a criminal. I could be." She said it as her chin went out. Daring him.

He laughed outright at the idea. "You're not a criminal," he countered, looking her up and down. "You're too cute."

Sierra knew too well that a sociopath could easily come across as charming and even normal. Her father was one of those people. He would order someone's death without a second thought and go about his day as if he'd just decided on spaghetti instead of lasagna for dinner. "So I'm a regular Bonnie Parker. What can I say?"

He laughed and bent even lower. "Can I be your Clyde Barrow? Minus all the killings, robberies and mayhem, of course."

She blushed, knowing that Bonnie and Clyde had a torrid love affair until they were both shot during an ambush. "I don't think we have the right personalities." She bowed her head so he couldn't see her blush.

He cocked his head to the side. "We definitely have the spark. Let's just take a go at it," he suggested.

She wasn't sure how to handle that since all she wanted to do was reach up and touch the dark part of his jaw, the part that looked like it still had a bit of stubble to it despite the use of a good razor only hours ago. "I have that meeting," she whispered, unable to make her voice stronger. "I really have to go now."

He didn't move away immediately, his eyes looking down at her and she suspected that he could read her mind, knew that she was both irritated and excited. "So you do," he finally said. With that, he stepped back and gave her space, his hands in his pockets as he watched her take a deep breath and knock on Todd's door.

"You can go on inside," Drake said from behind her.

Sierra glanced over her shoulder, not sure why he was telling her she could just barge into her boss's office. "Won't he...?"

"No." In fact, he opened the door for her, pushing the wooden door back so she could enter.

Sierra looked inside but the office was empty. Even most of the furniture was gone. "What's going on?" she asked cautiously, standing just inside the doorway.

She felt Drake right behind her, his chest against her shoulders as his hands settled on her hips. He looked into the office over her head as if he were seeing the space for the first time as well. "The movers did a good job," he said and gently pushed her inside, then closed the door behind the two of them. "Have a seat." He walked around her to one of the two chairs left in the room.

"What's happening?" she demanded, not taking the other chair. "Where's Todd and where is all of his furniture?" She'd always loved Todd's office. It was warm and grandfatherly. Not the style that would be conducive to her work, but it had felt warm and inviting.

Drake put his arm around her waist and brought her deeper into the room, closing the door behind the two of them. "Todd is already gone. He wanted to move on with his retirement as soon as possible. His wife was anxious that he might change his mind if given the chance to think about it and worry too much."

Sierra looked around, feeling sad, as if her boss moving on with his life was the end of an era. It was, in a way. Although she didn't want it to be the end of an era in her world. She liked her life. She wanted it to stay exactly the same. And that meant that this man was not in it!

Taking a deep breath, she turned around to face him, holding her notebook in front of her as if it could protect her. "I thought I was supposed to meet with Todd at nine o'clock."

His grin was her first indication that she'd been tricked. "No, you were only told to be in Todd's office at nine o'clock. There was no mention of who you would be meeting with."

Her eyes narrowed at his statement. "That was on purpose wasn't it?"

He chuckled softly. "Of course. I didn't want you running from the building in terror."

She straightened her shoulders, feeling uncomfortable with his description of her possible reaction. "I wouldn't do that."

He paused before he said, "Wouldn't you?"

She huffed and took the other seat but continued to hold her notebook in front of her like a shield. "Of course not. I'm a professional. So," she started off, "despite my already heavy workload, you said you had a special project for me. What is it?"

He looked at her long legs encased in the sleek, black slacks and her pretty, floral shoes with the killer heels. There was no way around it, this woman was beautiful, both inside and out. "I'll bet you wouldn't believe that I lured you in here to talk to me because I enjoy your company?" he teased.

She immediately snorted, her cynicism coming out strong and hard. "I look in the mirror. I'm not the raving beauties you normally date." She looked at him out of the corner of her eye. "I accept that you're out of my league. And I'm very thankful for that fact."

Drake studied her lovely features for a long moment, amazed that such a beautiful woman could be so unaware of her own appeal. "I'll just have to show you as we get to know each other then."

She crossed and uncrossed her legs, disagreeing with his confident statement. "Since we're not going to get to know each other, that's going to be rather difficult."

He grinned slowly. "There you go, throwing those challenges out to me. It must be that you don't understand my personality very well, which I'm more than willing to rectify."

"I don't want to get to know you."

"That's just your fear of what we feel for each other coming out. But I'm sure I can make you feel more comfortable about this attraction we have for each other. Given time, we'll both be comfortable."

Before she had a chance to contradict him, he launched into a discussion about a large project in a small area outside of Denver. It wasn't exactly a new city but it would be by the time he was finished with it. Over the past two years, he'd slowly purchased all of the buildings in a four street section in one of the run down areas of Denver. It was right on the outskirts of the up and coming section of the city, but still not a good place to be at night.

His plan was to renovate all the buildings, put in apartments, retail space, commercial offices as well as playgrounds, medical buildings and a community center.

As Sierra listened to Drake explaining it, even showing her the initial drafts of the layout, she was in awe of his vision. The man was literally taking apart a ghetto type area and replacing it with just about everything anyone could need. He even had agreements with the city to build a fire station and new police station next to the area, both of which would enormously increase the property values of the area.

"How did you get all of this land?" she asked.

He shrugged, looking down at the designs and Sierra could see the eagerness, the excitement in his eyes and even feel it in his body. "Most of the buildings were already for sale and at dirt cheap rates. It just took getting the other owners to sell as well, most of whom were more than eager to sell their burned out buildings to anyone who they considered stupid enough to buy them. Now, it's just a matter of getting things rolling. I'm guessing it will take approximately five years to finish all of the remodeling and rebuilding. Most of the buildings are structurally unsound.

What I want you to do is figure out which ones are salvageable and determine how to make them safe and which ones need to be just torn down and built over."

Sierra had never had such an opportunity and she was thrilled with the possibilities. Drake watched her lick her full, lower lip in anticipation as she slowly bent lower over the designs.

He almost groaned at the sight of her. He'd thought she was fascinating just when she was fighting this attraction between the two of them. Seeing her now though, bent over the designs, her eyes alight with all the ideas that were obviously pinging around in her head, he could barely contain his body's reactions.

They immediately started discussing the options, both of them tossing out ideas and they spent the rest of the day talking about possibilities, bringing other people into the conversation either in person because they were here in the office or calling them on the phone. Drake's assistant ordered lunch for them and Sierra didn't even mind sitting across from him while they devoured the meal because she was so interested, and hungry, and didn't want to leave the brainstorming session. At times, there were up to ten people in the office tossing around ideas and at other times, it was just the two of them bent over the plans, both of them with a pencil in their hand as they sketched out the various possibilities.

It was after ten o'clock that night when she finally stood up and realized what time it was. "Goodness," she gasped as she glanced at her watch. "I didn't realize that it was so late. I'd better head home," she said, obviously reluctant to leave. She quickly started picking up the Chinese food containers from their dinner, tossing them into the trash cans.

"Sorry for keeping you so late. Did you have plans for the evening?"

Sierra laughed and shook her head, tossing the broccoli and chicken away. "Definitely not."

"Why don't you have some eager guy waiting for you to get home in the evenings? Not that I mind, you understand. I definitely don't want any competition."

She shrugged, not exactly sure how to answer him. Honestly, she supposed. "I guess I get home from work too late most nights. I don't meet many men that are willing to put up with my schedule."

He looked at her closely. "There's more to it, isn't there?" He moved closer, drawn to her and he was glad when she didn't move away from him this time.

"I'm pretty private."

"I know that. Why is that?" he asked, moving even closer. There was that perfume again. It was so alluring, so soft and feminine. He knew he'd smelled it before, just couldn't place it. "You're young enough that you should be beating the men away. And you're amazingly beautiful."

Sierra took in a deep, shaky breath. "I don't..."

She didn't have a chance to reply. Drake didn't want to hear her excuses or denials of her beauty. And he was suddenly aware that her heart was racing and her breathing was erratic, sure signs that she was thinking along the exact same lines as he was.

When Drake's lips finally touched hers, Sierra was shocked at the intensity. Her knees wanted to give out on her, but the rest of her muscles decided that this was exactly what they wanted. And she found herself plastered against him, not because his hands were pulling her closer but because she wanted, needed, to get as close to him as possible. His mouth was demanding and she opened to him, eager for his kiss, his taste and his touch. She wanted him so badly and she was shaking with the intensity of her need.

When he pulled back slightly, looking down at her with a startled expression, she almost pulled back. "I don't..." she started to say, but she couldn't finish the sentence. Her hand reached up and pulled his head back down to hers, her mind going off in directions that wouldn't allow retreat.

She felt his hands on her waist, sliding up and caressing her softly, but not gently. His hands moved higher, slipping under her pink sweater and skimming along her skin, making her back arch so she was pressing herself more firmly against his touch.

When she felt his hands on her breasts, she couldn't stop the whimper of need that coursed through her. But she could beg him silently to do it again and when his thumb flicked against her nipple, she cried out, pulling away from him and looking up into his heated eyes with surprise.

"I can't do this," she whispered.

"You can," he contradicted and proved it by kissing her again, moving his hand against her breast and showing her how good it could feel. "Touch me, Sierra," he groaned as his fingers found the clasp of her bra and released it.

Sierra was frantically trying to unbutton the top buttons of his dress shirt, pushing his tie out of the way in her desperate need to touch his skin. She'd just gotten the first one undone when she heard a sound to her right.

"Oh!" a strange voice gasped.

Sierra looked over to her right, her eyes wide with both the need to touch him as well as the fear of someone in the firm discovering what they'd just been doing. And what they might be about to do.

She pulled her hands back, hearing his groan of frustration. Sierra knew exactly how he felt, but her need was dissipating quickly, replaced by the ever-present fear of this man. Both of what she wanted him to do to her as well as what he could do to her if he ever found out who she was.

Moments ago, she wouldn't have cared about her past or his. She would have reveled in the glorious feel of his hands touching her skin and begged for more of the same.

But with the interruption, reality returned. And that reality was painful and depressing.

"I have to go," she said abruptly, pulling her hands away from him and moving away, carefully stepping out of his arms and adjusting her clothing. Now that he wasn't touching her any longer, she could hear the steady hum of the vacuum cleaner as the janitorial staff worked their way through the offices. This was the second time that they'd saved her, sort of.

As she hurried down the hallway to grab her purse, she wondered how grateful she really was of their interruption. She might have wanted them to wait just a little longer.

"What's wrong?" Drake's voice asked from behind her and she spun around, her mouth open in surprise. She hadn't heard him follow her, but she should have anticipated that. He might be a great kisser and the sexiest man she'd ever laid eyes on, but he was also a gentleman. With resignation, she knew that he wouldn't allow her to walk out of the building alone.

"Nothing," she finally replied.

"Why is your face all flushed?" he asked softly, those incredibly intelligent eyes not missing anything.

"I need to hurry home," she said, not answering his question since it would give him so much more information than she wanted him to know about her and her current mental and physical state. Her control over her need was barely there and anything, even a gentle touch from him, might break that tenuous control.

He sighed and ran a hand over his face. "I know. I'll walk you out."

Sierra walked silently by his side, her whole body thrumming with the need for him to just take her into his arms, praying he might ignore her resistance and kiss her again. One simple kiss would bring them right back to where they'd been only ten minutes ago. One kiss would push all her fears out of her mind and she could....yes, she admitted that she wanted to make love with this man.

Impossible, she reprimanded herself. She couldn't do that to either of them.

At her car, she quickly pressed the lock release and slid into the driver's side. Before she could say anything else, she glanced up at him and forced herself to smile. "I'll see you at work next week," she stated clearly, telling him firmly that she wouldn't see him over the weekend. No, she'd maintain the mentally safe distance of the entire city of Denver in order to avoid him, get her mind back in control and her libido in check.

"Good night, Sierra," he said softly, not responding to her comment about next week in any way.

Sierra drove away, watching him through her rear view mirror as he stood in the parking lot watching her until she turned the corner.

She then focused all of her energy on driving home.

CHAPTER 4

Sierra pushed her hair off of her face with impatience, wishing she'd taken the time to pull it back. She couldn't figure out this tricky area and she needed to make this perfect. She wasn't going to admit to herself that she wanted to impress Drake with her ideas. They'd been working with each other for over a week now and things were moving quickly on the project, but even better, she'd been able to avoid any personal conversations with the man. It had been difficult the first few days because they'd been working on the project, but she'd been creative in her efforts, suspecting that he was even amused at times.

Her impatience now was only because this was a fantastic opportunity and she wanted to do it right. It could have a significant impact on her career so she couldn't mess this up.

"What are you doing here on a Saturday?" Drake's deep voice said from her office doorway.

Sierra spun around, her eyes widening as she took in his jeans and flannel shirt. She'd thought he looked great in a suit but boy! He looked especially sexy with the flannel pulled across his shoulders and jeans that weren't too tight but looked soft and well worn. Comfortable.

Couldn't the man wear a sack for her sake? And why was he here today? She was normally alone when she came into the office on the weekends.

She eyed him warily as he stood in the doorway, her mind flashing back to the kiss they'd shared last week. But she'd had several days to get over the impact of his kiss, she told herself. She could handle him today. She'd have to!

She sighed and pulled her eyes away from the man who had bothered her sleep for so many nights she was actually feeling sleep deprived. There were some moments lately that the only reason she was standing was because of coffee. "I'm trying to tweak some ideas I had last night."

Drake was no longer standing in her doorway but the only way she knew that was because he had walked over to stand beside her, his shoulders bumping her own and his large body causing a shadow to fall over her work. "From the designs you've submitted so far, I know you'll do an excellent job. What are you so worried about?" he asked, his finger running over the designs as he traced her changes.

She almost gasped at the image of his finger on her paper. Instantly, the thought of that same finger running down her arm or her leg, or even her stomach, caught her imagination and she couldn't think for a long moment. Couldn't even breathe.

When she didn't respond, he looked back at her, trying to find out what was wrong. But the look in her eyes, the softened mouth, lips that were slightly parted and the rapid rise and fall of her breasts under the soft, yellow sweater caused him to ignore the designs and turn to face her fully.

"Sierra, I'm going to kiss you," he said by way of a warning.

Sierra heard the words and knew from the last time he'd kissed her that she should pull away. She should run or at least tell him that she didn't want him to do anything to her, much less kiss her. But she couldn't move, couldn't stop him as his hands moved to her waist. She looked up at him, her eyes watching his progress as he slowly, so painfully slowly, lowered his head. Was he waiting for her to stop him? To push him away? She could no more stop him than he could stop the earth from spinning or the sun rising over the horizon each morning. It was as if this moment, this caress, was meant to happen and she'd been waiting for it ever since their last kiss. So much had happened, but it all came down to this kiss at this particular time.

She held her breath as she waited for his lips. When she felt them, their softness, the electrifying touch, she gasped, causing her to lean back slightly. His hands gripped her waist, holding her still, even pulling her closer. Her own hands were fisted into tight, tension filled balls, pressing against his biceps as if she were afraid to touch him. But as he deepened the kiss, her hands opened, her palms pressed against his arms, sliding higher, testing along the way.

And then her knees almost gave out on her when he stopped the gentleness. Her lack of resistance must have triggered something inside of him because he was no longer soft but demanding, no longer patient but commanding. His tongue invaded, took possession of her mouth and she melted against him, her body going up in flames of need while he continued to devour her.

She had no idea how it happened, but suddenly she was sitting on her work table, her legs around his waist and her hands sliding inside of his flannel shirt while his hands were moving up underneath her sweater impatiently.

When she felt his hands on her breasts she almost cried out, and would have if his mouth wasn't covering hers. But the sound she did make caused his head to come up and he looked down into her passion glazed eyes. His fingers weren't still though. They continued to cause her entire body to shiver, to shake with need and an almost painful desire that she didn't know how to control.

"We need to get out of here," he said, his voice deeper than normal and husky with his own desire. "Come back with me. We can finish this at my place."

It was exactly what she wanted, what she needed. But after the past week and all the trouble she'd had sleeping because thoughts of him kept filtering through her mind, she knew she shouldn't.

She shuddered, wanting him more than she thought was healthy. But she also knew that it wouldn't be a good idea. "I can't."

"Of course you can," he said and his hand went higher. She grabbed his wrist, closing her eyes to try and control the urges surging through her, but it was a tough battle.

"Drake, I can't do that."

With a sigh, he leaned his forehead against hers. "You're killing me, you know that right?"

She laughed softly, relieved that he wasn't angry with her for rejecting his suggestion. "It's better this way."

"Better for who? And if you aren't coming home with me, you have to let go of me."

She looked startled and pulled her head back, then realized he was talking about her legs which were still tightly wrapped around his hips. "Oh!" she gasped and let her legs drop down.

He wasn't as fast about moving away from her and she shivered when she realized what was plastered against her stomach. She looked up at him, his eyes laughing down at her when she blushed with the realization. "Yes, you affect me that much," he confirmed.

She was both embarrassed and turned on by his statement. He was so earthy, taking his sexuality as if it were normal and natural. She'd always been embarrassed by the idea of sex but Drake didn't allow any sort of embarrassment. It was what it was and he accepted that as a part of his life.

On the other hand, she had been brought up to think of sex as something to be avoided at all costs. She was to remain a virgin until her wedding night and even after that, it was implied that she should only have sex for procreation. It wasn't stated so much as just grunted whenever her father had even broached the subject of sex. "Don't let a man touch you!" he'd arbitrarily say while passing her or her sister Marissa in the hallways. Or over dinner, "Make sure your dates keep their hands to themselves! Or I'll make sure they don't touch anyone else. Got it?"

She and her sister had sometimes chuckled at his adamant stand on sexual encounters, but until this moment, she'd never understood how deeply ingrained her father's words had gone into her subconscious. Of course, no man had ever gotten close enough to her for her to even consider that aspect of her personality.

As they separated, Drake kept a sharp eye on her. "Okay, you're not going to come home with me so I can make love to you for the rest of the day and well into the night. I'll accept that for now," he said but kept close, leaving barely an inch between their bodies. "However, I'm not going to allow you to stay here and work all day. There are much more important things to do with a Saturday." With that, he took her hand and pulled her out of her office.

Sierra glanced back at her drafting board, her eyes looking at the plans with longing because they were safe and didn't have a dangerous history. They were benign while Drake was anything but! "I really need to work out this detail," she tried to argue, but his good humor was just too infectious.

He pressed the elevator button then leaned against the wall, pressing against her and smiling when her eyes widened with surprise. "Nope. A brain needs time to recuperate after a long work week and you've been spending too many hours in the office." He stopped and looked down at her. "I've been watching you." He said it with mock seriousness, but she could tell that, underneath his humor, he was serious. What he might have been watching was up for debate but she'd prefer to keep it innocent. Especially since her body was still singing with anticipation after that last kiss.

"I don't think...."

"No way. I've been watching you and you' are going to burn out. You're coming with me today," he ordered as they walked out of the elevator and pressed the security button that would release the lock on the lobby doorway. "And stop arguing. This will be perfect for you." He looked her up and down. "The jeans will work, but you can't wear that sweater."

His hands started to reach for her and Sierra laughed when she thought he might just take off her sweater. "Don't you dare," she ordered, pointing at him with a warning finger. He didn't acknowledge her warning tone though. He simply took her finger in his hand and pulled her closer.

"You know I love it when you dare me to do something. You're pretty cute, but daring me only makes me more determined."

She laughed again, thinking he was teasing her. But when one of his eyebrows went up, she thought he might be serious, which only made her laugh harder. "Okay, warning taken, absorbed and processed."

"Good. So now let's figure out what we're going to do with your inappropriate clothing choices."

She looked down at her simple sweater and her neat pair of jeans, both of which were perfectly appropriate for working on a Saturday. "What's wrong with my clothes?"

He leered at her. "Besides the fact that they aren't laying on the floor beside my bed?" he asked her. He didn't wait for an answer but continued, "Well, they simply won't work for what we're going to do today."

She ignored his comment about the first part of his statement and focused on the second part. "I was perfectly content working in the office. So as far as I'm concerned, my clothes are fine." She crossed her arms over her chest and jutted out her chin, but there was still amusement in her eyes.

He grinned slightly, his eyes glancing down. With her arms like that, it pushed her breasts up higher, showing him just a touch of cleavage. "You're cute when you get all stubborn like that. I like it."

She rolled her eyes. "And you're avoiding my question."

It was a bright, sunny day with the fresh, fall air making everything seem possible. "It rained last night," he said and opened the door to a big, brown truck. "The conditions are perfect for what I have planned today." With that, he lifted her into the seat of the truck and slammed the door shut.

When he pulled himself up into the driver's seat, she couldn't stop her eyes from noticing his broad shoulders and those muscular thighs once again. "Where's the black car you were driving last night?" she asked, only slightly flustered because of his hands on her waist and images of those shoulders without the flannel shirt covering them. She considered that progress and was gaining confidence about being around him.

As Sierra fastened her seatbelt, she was struck by how eager, excited he was by whatever he had planned for today. When he got inside next to her, she looked at him cautiously. "What are your plans today?"

"My priority today," he stopped as he turned over the engine and shrugged slightly, "well, my priority every day lately is to have you screaming out my name as we make love together. But since that's on the back burner for the moment," he ignored her attempt to interrupt him as he continued, "we're going out to the tracks."

He expertly maneuvered the enormous truck through the parking lot. Tracks? A racetrack? Why would she need to change out of her sweater simply to attend a racetrack? "What do you mean? What tracks are you going to?"

He grinned at her attempt to distance herself from his plans. "You're coming with me so stop using the term as if I'm leaving you behind. You're going to love this. I promise."

"If I'm going to love it so much, why won't you tell me what's going on? And why did you feel the need to wait until we're on the highway before you give me any kind of clue except that my clothes aren't appropriate? That could mean anything from needing a ball gown to a bathing suit."

He glanced over at her and she instantly saw the salacious thought racing through his mind. "A bathing suit sounds like a great idea. I'll have to work that into my plans. Unfortunately, I hadn't thought of that in advance or I'd have gotten you out to the beach somewhere."

She sighed and shook her head. "Okay, so no bathing suit. Where are we going?" He was certainly in a playful mood today. And his mood was contagious. She was quickly becoming entranced by this new side to him. She'd seen the serious and lover-like Drake. She'd experienced his teasing and business personalities too. But with all the power he wielded, she never would have suspected this playful, eager man to show up. If it weren't for his rugged, handsome face and the enormous muscles all over his body, this Drake could pass for a little boy.

"Tell me what you were working on. You seemed pretty frustrated when I walked in on you."

She started to open her mouth to explain what she'd been trying to work into the plans but then stopped herself. She wanted to do this on her own. Drake was a genius and if she started to explain, he would simply tell her how to fix the challenge she was facing. She didn't want that. She wanted to figure it out on her own. "No. I'm not telling you anything."

"Why not?" He eyed her curiously as he expertly controlled the truck.

She glanced outside the big windows of the cab, impressed with how high off of the street they were inside this truck. They were now heading outside the city into the foothills. This was only mildly concerning because there were lots of fun places to explore outside of Denver but she had no idea what "tracks" might be located out in this direction. The spaces outside of the city were beautiful in a rugged, sometimes dangerous way. There were lots of things to do outdoors if one could leave the buildings behind. That would also explain why her clothes were inappropriate. She was definitely not dressed for hiking through the mountains.

She turned back to face him, cheekily grinning at him across the expanse of the interior. "Because you'll figure out how to get it fixed and I want to im…" she stopped before she could finish. "Before I have to show it to anyone," she finished lamely. She didn't look at him to see if he'd caught her slip, but she cringed because Drake never missed anything.

"Okay, so you want to impress me with your creativity. That's great," he said and winked at her when she glared at him. "But I'm already impressed. You've used some interesting materials that I wouldn't have thought about so anything you do from here on out is going to further impress me with your skills."

She almost glowed with his compliment. She wanted to ask him what materials he was surprised about but she didn't want to emphasize the issue too much. It might make him think that she cared about his opinion too much and that could put her in an awkward position.

She sighed out loud, wishing things could be different. Why was life so complicated? Why couldn't she and Drake just be friends? Why did he have to make everything into this uncomfortable, mind numbing craziness that made her lose control? She didn't like that feeling, didn't understand it. And even if she could ignore her anxiousness about the way he made her feel, she couldn't betray him.

She looked over at him, impressed with the way he handled the increasingly rugged roads, his strong hands and long fingers confident on the steering wheel, his tall, muscular body relaxed as he drove. She should just tell him who she was. She should be honest with him. Was she being dishonest by not admitting that her father had beaten him and left him to die?

"No long faces today," he told her firmly as he glanced quickly in her direction. "Today is a non-stress day."

She had to laugh at his command. "You're dictating that I can't feel any stress at all? For the next twenty-four hours?"

"Absolutely," he grinned arrogantly at her. "Unless it is stress I've created because I'm touching you and you want more. That's perfectly acceptable stress."

She laughed, feeling more confident with him on the other side of the big truck and a large console between them. She wouldn't feel so confident if he were right next to her saying those kinds of things.

But his words did help her make a decision. She would have fun with him today, finish her project tonight at home and then talk to him on Monday morning, admit to everything her father had done and then move on with her life.

He'd probably fire her, she thought with more than a touch of sadness. And she knew he would be completely justified. One didn't continue to employ the daughter of one's murderer, even if it turned out to be an attempted murder.

"Want to talk about it?" he asked, reaching out and taking her hand which had been laying on the console.

She felt the heat in his fingers and shivered when his thumb rubbed against her knuckles. "You're right. We'll just enjoy the day. We can talk about stressful issues on Monday."

"That's the spirit!" he replied, squeezing her hand.

He pulled off of the highway onto a road that didn't appear to be much of a road. There were no signs of any life this far outside of the city but people who lived out this far preferred their space. "Where are we going?" she asked, interested despite her wariness. They were leaving the urban world behind and climbing the mountains, the trees turning to pines as they went deeper into the woods.

He didn't answer, but simply made another left onto what she wasn't sure was actually a road. Or not a truck worthy one. "Okay, now you have to tell me what's going on," she said as the trees blocked out the sunshine.

"I 'have to'?" he asked, looking at her with amusement lacing those intense eyes. "Why do I 'have to' tell you? And what are you going to do to make me tell you?" He leered at her with sexual innuendo. "I think I'll enjoy you trying to torture the information out of me."

Sierra bit her lower lip as another shiver of awareness laced through her. So much for the extra space and her ability to control what he made her feel! She tried to pull her hand away, but he wouldn't relinquish her fingers. "Drake, where are we going?"

He shook his head, thinking she looked adorable as she sat almost next to him, worried and anxious that he'd just kidnapped her. It wasn't a bad idea, he thought. Being out here for the whole weekend, he might just get her to admit why she was so hot for him one moment, and then pulling away from him with fear in her eyes the next. "Nope. Just a few more minutes and you'll see. It's right around the corner."

"What's around the corner?" she asked with impatience. She hated not knowing a secret. It drove her crazy and she even had to shake Christmas and birthday presents to try and figure out what was inside the boxes.

And then she gasped when the truck climbed up a particularly steep incline. She gripped the door handle and his own hand, not even aware of how tightly she was gripping his fingers. Her body was even turning towards him in an effort to stay away from the drop beside her window. "I guess this is a good time to tell you that I don't really like heights."

He glanced over at her, all amusement gone when he saw her genuine fear. This wasn't about what they meant to each other or what he could make her feel. The fear in her eyes was all about something stronger and scarier. "Don't worry," he said with a strong, reassuring tone of voice, squeezing her fingers again to help her. "I've done this trip many times. This truck can handle the road."

Sierra didn't have his confidence. In fact, if it weren't for her seatbelt holding her in her seat, she might actually climb onto the console to get away from the cliff on her side of the truck. The road seriously didn't look like it was wide enough to accommodate this huge truck and if it did, there wasn't any room for error.

A moment later, he pulled around a corner and she breathed a sigh of relief. Then gasped in pleasure at the amazing house perched on the side of the mountain. "Oh my," she sighed, her eyes taking in the complex architectural structure. She'd read about this place in the architectural magazines but it was even more astounding in reality than in the pictures. The photographer hadn't really captured the amazing structure. The house seemed to be balanced with cantilevers on both sides, using the mountain as part of its structure. There were walls of windows on three sides with large, metal columns holding up the jutting end of the house.

"This is magnificent," she breathed. "I've always wanted to design something like this for a client."

"Why haven't you?" he asked, unsnapping his seatbelt while he watched her.

She shrugged as she too got out, her eyes never leaving the house that looked like it was dangerously perched on the mountain, about to slide down the cliff at any moment. But her eyes noted the sound structure, the impressive way the designer had stabilized the house and she instantly fell in love.

"Because my clients haven't wanted it," she sighed with happiness just to view the building. "I think I'm going to marry the man who designed this."

Drake watched carefully as Sierra walked around the truck. He was leaning against the hood of the truck, his arms crossed over his chest in an attempt to not pull her into his arms and kiss her. Hell, he wanted to make love to her right here, uncaring of the rocks or gravel. She might object, he thought. Well, actually, she objected to any kind of touch from him most of the time.

He smiled as he clarified his thought. She only objected to his touch before and after he touched her. She never objected during the actual physical contact. In fact, she was a tigress when it came to touching him back.

Damn, he liked that about her. Not the resistance. No, that was something he'd have to eliminate completely from her. He much preferred the sensuous beauty she was when she was in his arms versus the straight-laced, tense woman she was when she was avoiding his touch.

And marry the person who had designed the house? He liked the idea. He liked that a lot. As he watched her look at his house from different angles, he couldn't help but admire her long legs in those tight jeans giving him a glimpse of her adorable butt and her trim waist. He would prefer her hair down around her shoulders, but she'd probably need it pulled back for what he had in mind today.

Tonight though. He'd have that hair down around her shoulders tonight.

"Come on inside. I'll get you a different shirt. That sweater won't help you a lot for what I have planned."

Sierra pulled her eyes away from the house, her attention captured by the man and his comment. "What do you have planned?"

He took her hand and pulled her along, tucking her hand onto his arm and then covering it with his other hand to keep her from pulling it away. This kept her closer and she kept bumping his hips as she walked quickly to keep up with him.

"I'll lend you one of my shirts. That should cover enough of you."

She blinked as she looked up at him, curiosity getting the better of her common sense. She knew she should tell him to just go ahead with his plans and she'd be happy to wander around inside his house. She wouldn't mind spending an hour simply investigating the support system built by the architect.

But she couldn't help the question that escaped her. "Why do I need a shirt big enough to cover me?" Despite herself, she was intrigued by both his comment as well as his excited expression.

"Because we're going to get a bit dirty today." He unlocked the front door of the house and led her straight through the great room and into a hallway. She tried to get a glimpse of the house but only got the impression of comfortable furniture, soaring ceilings and magnificent views.

"I'll take you on a tour of the place when we are finished," he said, chuckling at her as she strained her neck to get a better view of his house.

When he led her into a large bedroom, she sighed with awe of the view. She didn't see the extremely large bed or the furniture that looked like it should be in a museum. All she saw was the mountains and the city spread out below. There was definitely a different feeling when one looked down from the mountains versus being inside of a tall building. She couldn't quite define it, but the view was exceptional.

She stood in the middle of his bedroom, unaware that he'd released her hands and had disappeared into a closet. He came out a moment later and just stood about six feet away watching her as she stood enjoying the view. He admired her for several moments before he glanced at his watch. With a chuckle, he walked over to her. "Want some help taking off the sweater?" he asked, holding the large, flannel shirt up in front of her eyes.

Sierra looked at the shirt, confused and nervous. "Definitely not. I can take off my sweater by myself." She took the shirt and glared up at him.

Drake shrugged and sat down on the bed, waiting. "Go ahead."

Sierra took a step back. "I'm not doing a striptease for you," she stated firmly.

Drake's eyes went up and down her slender figure. "Pity," was all he said. With a grin, he nodded towards the wall. "There's a bathroom over there if you insist on being modest."

She looked at the wall and saw the door. Turning towards it, she almost tripped when she heard him say, "I'm going to see it all pretty soon anyway."

She glanced back at him, her eyes wide with the fear that idea generated. And the heat.

How could he do this to her so easily? She almost slammed the bathroom door shut, slamming out his laughing, too-knowing eyes. Leaning against the door, she took several deep breaths, unaware that she was clutching his shirt to her chest until she opened her eyes to try and figure out why she could still smell the man's spicy cologne. When she realized what she was doing, she relaxed her hold, but then brought the shirt up to her face, breathing in the clean, wonderful scent.

She pushed herself away from the wall and pulled her pink sweater over her head. When she slipped her arms into the flannel shirt, it was more of a dress than a shirt. The ends hung down to almost her knees and her arms were swallowed up in the fabric. She had to roll up the arms several times before her hands could peek out the ends of the sleeves. Taking the tails, she gathered them up and tied them in a knot around her waist.

Feeling more than a little ridiculous, she opened the door to the bathroom once again. She found him staring out at the view but at the first sound of her coming out, he swung around to watch her.

Her step faltered when she saw the heat in his eyes as he took in her smaller frame wearing his clothes. "What?" she asked, her fingers nervously tightening the knot around her waist.

"You look hot in my shirt," he finally explained. He came closer, his hands resting on her hips as he looked down at her. "Of course, you'd look sexier without it."

She rolled her eyes and would have stepped out of his arms but he wouldn't let her. "What now?" she asked.

His body language changed slightly. Subtly. "It just occurred to me that I have you here in my bedroom. I've pictured you here so many times its almost hard to resist the urge to lift you up and carry you over to my very comfortable, very large bed and have my wicked way with you." He instantly felt her body stiffen and he controlled himself with difficulty. "I won't," he assured her softly. "But only because you're going to love what I have planned. And if I get you into that bed, it will be a long time before I actually allow you to leave it."

She couldn't relax, not with those words hanging in the air. Even though he'd assured her that they would be doing something else, she still bit her lip with...indecision?

Surely not, she admonished herself. But she let out the breath she'd been holding when he took her hand and led her out of the bedroom.

CHAPTER 5

He shortened his stride to allow her to keep up with him more easily as he led her back out into the crisp, mountain air. When he walked both of them over to a garage in the back of the house, she still didn't understand what he had planned for the day. But when the garage door opened to reveal two tough looking all-terrain vehicles, Sierra quickly started shaking her head and backing up.

With a laugh, she said, "Drake, there is no way I'm riding on one of those."

He ignored her and pushed one of them out into the sunshine. "It's much easier than you might think."

She eyed the four wheeled machine dubiously. "And a whole lot scarier, I'm sure." She didn't think there was anything he could say to her that would prove these vehicles were not only safe, but a good way to spend a Saturday afternoon. "They look like death traps."

He smiled but shook his head. "Not at all. These vehicles grip the road pretty well and I promise I won't take you on any challenging slopes. At least not this time. The steering on my ATVs is much more responsive than on the ones you might have driven somewhere else. So they're easier to handle on the corners." He stuffed some bags into the machine's holding areas and looked up at her.

"I've never driven one, good or bad steering, so that kind of reassurance isn't going to help me get onto that vehicle, Drake." She stood there staring at him as if he'd lost his mind. He must have if he thought she would enjoy riding on something so vulnerable. It was almost like a motorcycle, but with extra wheels.

"They are steady and a lot of fun, I promise. You'll love it if you only give it a try."

She still stood back away from the machine, crossing her arms and shaking her head. "You can try and convince me all you want, but it simply isn't going to happen."

She felt the trembling in her knees the moment she saw the victory in his eyes. He shrugged and pushed the vehicle out of the garage further, looking over the engine carefully. "If you don't want to drive one, that's fine. I can deal with that."

She should have relaxed with his assurance, but something about the way he was accepting her resistance worried her.

A few minutes later, her wariness was confirmed. With the engine revving, he pulled on a helmet, then tossed one to her. She caught it in her fingers, but only looked at it as if it were a foreign concept. "What am I supposed to do with this?" she asked, bracing herself for whatever he was planning.

"Put it on." He grinned and revved the engine one more time.

With a grin on his handsome face that she could only describe as pure triumph, she started to step back. His shaking head was her only warning before she somehow found herself on the back of the ATV while he sped off. He hadn't tried to cajole her or give her a long list of statistics about the safety or power of the ATV. He'd simply lifted her off of her feet, ignoring her laughing objections and plunked her onto the back of the double seat. He then threw his own leg over the seat, effectively trapping her and he revved the engine a moment before he released the break. Taking off with a spewing of gravel and his grin of excitement.

She gripped the helmet with her fingers while her hands held onto his shoulders. She was sitting behind him so it was hard to see where he was going, but she could see from both sides of him and the land was whizzing by them.

"You're going to need to hold onto me more tightly," he said as he slowed down to turn a corner.

As quickly as her numb fingers could move, she strapped the helmet on, latching it below her chin. She was glad she'd done that quickly though when he whipped around a tree and then pushed the power on the ATV. The wheels ground through the mud as it steadily climbed a very narrow mountain trail.

Sierra panicked as she looked around, but as he continued to expertly maneuver around the trails, she started to relax. And amazingly, she was actually enjoying the ride while she hugged his waist. She became excited every time he sped up or rounded a particularly dangerous looking corner. Within only a few minutes, she was pointing to different areas, encouraging him to drive in one direction or another and she laughed with thrilling exhilaration as he pushed the machine to go faster or climb higher.

Drake wasn't sure if he would be able to maintain his control throughout the ride. Each time he turned a corner, he felt her soft breast against his back, her soft breath against his shoulder when she laughed and her thighs pressing against his hips. He'd suspected that she would like riding the ATVs, but he'd had no idea how much she'd like it. She was completely into the danger now. And he was both loving her excitement and gritting his teeth against the lust surging through his body with her softness pressed so firmly against his back.

When he felt her grip around him loosen, he knew that it was probably time to stop. She had to be worn out. "Are you hungry?" he asked, turning slightly so his voice would carry above the sound of the engine.

"Starving!" she called back to him.

He nodded, and then turned the vehicle towards the south, heading down a barely-there pathway. When they reached his destination, he turned off the engine and let her enjoy the majesty of the view in silence.

"Wow," she sighed, looking out at the mountains laid out in front of her.

"I know. Pretty amazing, isn't it?"

He stepped off of the ATV and went to the back, unsnapping some industrial strength hooks on the sides of the machine. The back area of the vehicle was actually a place to carry things and Drake pulled out a bag. Sierra watched, her mouthwatering as he spread out a blanket on one of the warm rocks, then handed her a sandwich and lemonade. There were also bags of chips and some decadent cookies but Sierra curled her legs underneath her and accepted the sandwich and drink gratefully. "This is delicious," she gushed as she bit into the tomato and mozzarella sandwich with some sort of spicy, tangy spread. "Who made this?"

"I did," he replied as if that were the most obvious thing in the world.

She eyed him out of the corner of her eye. "Are you sure you didn't buy this at some fancy grocery store? Cooking just doesn't seem like an activity you would enjoy."

"I love cooking actually. It's pretty relaxing. My housekeeper continues to find different ingredients for me. I like the challenge of coming up with something interesting to make with each of her finds."

She wasn't sure that she believed him, but she didn't really feel like arguing about the issue on such a beautiful day. "So how long have you owned the house?" she asked, changing the subject.

Drake almost laughed out loud at her. She was sitting near him looking extremely prim and proper, completely disbelieving that he might know how to cook, even though he'd cooked a delicious pasta meal for her just over a week ago. Did she think that had been a fluke?

Deciding to humor her, he said, "I bought the land about six or seven years ago. The house was only finished maybe three years ago." He'd just have to show her tonight how well he cooked when he had her back at his house. While he watched her and answered her questions, his mind thought about the different things he might prepare for dinner. And all the things he would do to her before and after their meal.

"Why did it take you so long to finish the house?" she asked, wondering if he'd had financial problems after his hospitalization. She couldn't outright ask him about that though. Not without revealing her connection. Monday, she promised herself. She'd tell him all about her past and her father's criminal history on Monday.

"Initially, I was wrapped up in a personal project and couldn't take the time away from that to focus on building this house," he explained, his mind flashing back to his crusade to imprison the man who had beaten him almost to death. He'd delegated almost all of his duties that year so he could focus only on finding evidence that would put Joe Berutelli into prison. He didn't want to tell that to Sierra. She looked like she might faint just at being in that man's presence. He didn't want her to know that he'd basically put his life in danger on several occasions in order to get back at the sociopath. "I couldn't find an architect who knew how to do what I wanted to do." It had all worked out in the end. The man had been murdered after a quick murder trial of his own. That trial had resulted in Joe Berutelli finally been put behind bars without possibility of parole. Drake felt no guilt that the man had himself been murdered in prison by one of his enemies.

That was in the past and he was here with the most beautiful woman he'd ever seen in his life as she sat primly on the blanket across from him, nibbling at her sandwich while he made plans for their night together.

He had a slight pang of guilt over the memory of the woman from the hospital. Once he'd gotten Joe Berutelli taken care of, he'd worked hard to track down the woman who had saved his life. Not just once by calling for paramedics after he'd been dumped in a filthy alley. But throughout his long recovery, he remembered feeling her sit close to him, her hand touching his arm and her voice begging him to fight the pain, to fight and return to the world. Her voice had been vague and her face always fuzzy because of the incredible pain he'd gone through so he never had a very good look at her.

Unfortunately, by the time he'd finished with Berutelli and come back to find his mystery woman, the trail had gone cold. No one at the hospital could give him anything but vague descriptions of the woman. Besides blue eyes and long, brown hair, all they could say was that she was pretty, painfully thin and always looking sad.

Drake pushed thoughts of the stranger out of his mind. He'd searched for her for so long without any trace of her. At times, he thought she might have been a figment of his imagination. He needed to give up the hope of finding her, especially since he'd found Sierra. And there was no way he was going to lose her.

Yes, his luck at finding this stunningly sensuous woman was proof that it was time for him to move on with his life.

Starting tonight. He chewed on his sandwich while his eyes moved over her tiny waist where his shirt was knotted, her long legs encased in those tight jeans that were now covered in dust. Even her porcelain skin looked dusty and darker with flecks of mud splattering her high cheekbones but he thought she looked delicious!

She stopped before taking her next bite of her sandwich, not sure she understood what he was telling her. "Are you saying that you basically designed the house?"

He focused back on the conversation, pushing the past where it belonged. "Yes." He winked at her shock. "I'm going to hold you to that marriage proposal earlier."

She ignored his teasing and stared at him. "So you knew what you wanted to do but no one knew how to create it?"

"Sort of. Everyone kept telling me that it was impossible."

"But the cantilever. It's been done before. Decades ago, actually. There's a house in Pennsylvania by Frank Lloyd Wright that basically does the same thing."

"I know. I visited the site several times."

She looked at him with blatant confusion. "So why was it so difficult to find an architect to do the designs?"

"Because no one is as smart as you are about cantilevers and support systems."

She almost reared back with that compliment, so surprised by the sincerity. "But…"

"Give it up, Sierra. You're more daring than the others." He winked at her, enjoying her blush at his sincere compliment.

She looked at the view, her mind racing. "I was still in college when you built the house."

"Yes. I didn't catch wind of your work until about a year ago. Which is when I started negotiating on the project you're on now."

She bit her lip and looked down, her appetite completely gone with the rush of amazement that washed over her. "That's very nice of you."

He looked at her curiously, his eyes squinting slightly in the sunshine. "You don't take compliments very well, do you? But rest assured, I wanted you on this team from the beginning but my research showed me that you were too loyal to Todd. So I worked it out so that I could get you on the team that will build the next city area, with interesting twists and creative ideas. You're an original, Sierra. Just accept it."

"There are other architects out there that are more talented."

"There are others out there that are just as talented and just as skilled, but I like your preferences. It's sort of similar to going to a restaurant. Italian food might be extremely good, but if you don't like Italian, you're going to dine at the Mexican restaurant. Everyone has their own flair, their own preferences. I think your preferences and mine are similar. So I got you on the team."

She blushed and had to look away. "I'm flattered."

71

He grabbed the bag of chips, eagerly taking one out and tossing it into his mouth. "You should be. I only hire the best. Eat up," he ordered sternly, changing the subject once again and alleviating some of the tension that had come up with her embarrassment. "I'm not an easy boss. So you might be wishing I'd left Todd's firm alone."

She took another bite of her sandwich, feeling enormously better about the whole world. Simply because this man liked her work? That seemed slightly silly. Others had complimented her work before. She'd even been written up in several architectural journals and asked to speak at conferences. She'd turned down the speaking offers, preferring to continue working instead of talking about her work. But nothing compared to the simple statement from Drake.

"So tell me why you wanted to be an architect," he asked, opening the box of cookies.

"You can't have cookies now," she laughed, relieved when he changed the subject.

"Why not?"

"Because you just had chips."

He shrugged his shoulders. "And?"

She rolled her eyes as if he were being silly. "And…eating a cookie means that you're finished with lunch. That means I get the bag of chips. Toss it here."

He caught on at that point, slowly shaking his head. "If you want the chips, you have to come over and get them."

She looked him up and down and shook her head. "You're not going to be a gentleman and hand them over?" she asked, wiping her hands on a napkin. She surveyed him carefully, wondering how she could get the bag of chips delicately without ending up in a genuine tussle with him. He was too big and too strong. She'd definitely lose any physical fight she picked with him.

She tried to maintain a straight face, but she was pretty sure he wasn't buying it. So with a glance over his shoulder, she turned away. Then quickly turned back around, squinting her eyes at some point over his shoulder. With a shake of her head, she stopped looking, then glanced right back to the spot where her eyes had been.

Once again, she shook her head, then shielded her eyes as if she were trying to see something far away.

"What is it?" he asked, his expression indicating that he didn't quite believe her.

Sierra knew she had to take more drastic actions. She put her half-eaten sandwich down on the plastic wrapper and stood up, still shielding her eyes as she looked out over the horizon. Biting her lip seemed like a good idea because it added

72

to her look of anxiety but also kept her from smiling when he started to buy into the problem.

"Sierra? What's going on? Do you see something?" he asked, shifting around to try and see what she was concerned about. He shielded his eyes, scanning the horizon himself.

Sierra knew she'd never have another chance. With nimble fingers and a racing heart, she grabbed the bag of chips and took off in the opposite direction. Regrettably, she was laughing so hard she couldn't run fast enough. Drake realized what she was up to more quickly than she was expecting. Within seconds, he was up and chasing after her.

If she had been more creative, she might have thought about getting him a bit farther away from the pilfered chips. But as it was, he was quick as lightening and was only inches from her within seconds. Before she knew it, he grabbed her around the waist and she screamed out, laughing at her pathetic attempt to steal potato chips.

Her hair was flying around her face, blocking out her ability to see what he was doing but she felt the world spin around slightly. She was also laughing so hard she could barely breathe, gasping for breath. She tried to hold his hands away, but he was so much stronger and much more agile. He had the chip bag away from her as soon as he had her on the blanket, holding them above her body in a taunting fashion.

"Are you going to apologize for trying to steal the chips?" he demanded, one hand holding her down and tickling her while the other arm continued to hold the chips over her head. Because his arms were longer, she couldn't even reach them when she tried to grab them. But she was still laughing too hard and it also required two hands to try and stop his other hand from tickling her. She had no strength though because of the laughter which was sapping all of her energy. No matter how much she wiggled, she simply couldn't get out from underneath him or avoid his tickling hand.

"No!" she yelled out, still trying to grab his wrists. "You're a chip hog and I stole them because you were taunting me."

"Well, I'm still taunting you. What are you going to do about it now?"

She giggled uncontrollably, even trying to roll over onto her stomach to get away from his nimble hands. "Stop!" she begged. But he easily flipped her back, grabbing both of her arms in his free hand and holding them over her head.

That was when Sierra knew she was really in trouble. Her laughter died and her breathing was still heavy, but now for a completely different reason. Her body was suddenly very aware of his larger frame over hers, his hips pressing against hers. Even as she looked up at him, she felt his body's reaction to their closeness and her pulse skyrocketed.

73

"I want you," he said softly but with an urgency that had been controlled before.

"It can't work," she replied but it was hard for her to remember why it wouldn't work. In fact, it was painfully difficult for her to remember that she didn't really like this man, didn't want to deal with his arrogance and confidence. At this particular moment, she couldn't remember that they were not meant to have a relationship because right at this moment, all she wanted was for the moment to go on and on. And to have him bend down and kiss her, to feel his lips against hers.

When he finally did that, she lifted her head to meet him as much as she could with her arms pinned above her head. When he felt her lips quiver under his, his hands released hers and came down to cradle her head. He tried to be gentle, but it was difficult when she was kissing him back just as passionately. Aware of his size against her slender figure, he rolled off of her but pulled her to his side, his leg shifting ever so slightly so that one of his was in between hers. His hand reached down and pulled her knee, cradling his hardness against her hips.

He almost groaned when he felt her hands on his head, her fingers gently tugging at his hair, begging him without words to come closer. She shifted her legs, pressing her own hips closer, finding his hardness and thrilling him with her eagerness to be close to him. His hands shifted her, pulling her harder against him and one hand slid underneath the flannel shirt, finding the soft, delicate skin underneath.

With a groan, he pulled back and looked down at her. "We have to go back to my place to continue this," he said and stood up quickly, reaching down to give her a hand as well. "Unfortunately, I didn't bring any protection with me." When she put her hand into his, he almost lifted her up when he pulled her into his arms to kiss her once again, deeply, while his hands went to her hips and pulled her closer again. "You feel incredible! I can't believe I wasn't prepared for this. Let's go."

CHAPTER 6

He was already bending down and stuffing the blanket and food items back into the bag, preparing to store them in the back of the ATV when her senses came back to her.

"Wait," she said when he lifted her up, about to carry her along to the back of the bike. "What are we doing?" she asked, her hands braced on his shoulders.

"We're going back to my place. Then I'm going to carry you into my bedroom," he kissed her, putting her onto the seat of the ATV and lifting his own leg to straddle the seat backwards before bending low over her as he kissed her again and again. "And then I'm going to make love to you as we were doing moments ago."

He'd already stuffed the picnic materials into the holder when his words sunk in. "Wait, we can't do that." She was shaking from the impact of both his words and the need to do exactly what he'd said. She wanted nothing more than to make love with this man but they couldn't do that. There was too much between them, too much history and she couldn't do that to him.

She'd forgotten that she didn't like him. His eagerness, the excitement, his humor and so many other things had obliterated her irritation with his arrogance and his high-handed nature. After today, that no longer mattered. Besides, he wasn't acting arrogant and conceited now. He was sweet and kind and gentle. And fun! He was a different person out here in the wilderness than he was in the office. She liked this man. She'd laughed with him and he'd made her relax. She hadn't had a great deal of that in her life so far and she didn't want to ruin it by having sex with him. Not with this dreaded secret she'd been keeping from him.

He stilled and looked at her worried features. With a deep sigh, he came back to stand in front of her. "Tell me what's wrong, Sierra. Because what we were just doing felt extremely right."

She bit her lip, unsure of what to say, how to convey her regret without telling him everything.

"There are things about me that you don't know about. My past isn't...nice," was all she could say. She tried to tell him everything, knowing that he deserved the truth. But something held her back. A look in his eyes, the patience and kindness she'd suspected before, but hadn't ever witnessed. It was probably the perfect time, but she simply couldn't form the words.

His work-roughened hand came up to caress her cheek and she closed her eyes to keep herself from leaning into his hand and giving him yet another mixed message. "Okay, so you're not ready to tell me what's holding you back. We've only known each other for a short period of time and you need to know more about me. You don't fully trust me yet."

That wasn't it, she thought silently with misery overwhelming her. "Actually," she said as she twisted her fingers together, "you need to know me better. There are a lot of things about me that you might not like."

He almost laughed out loud at the idea of this sweet, gentle, intelligent woman having a past that could be so horrible. "So tell me now. I can look at your lips that are still soft and swollen and that might counter any anger I'll have with you for whatever heinous crimes you've committed in the past."

He was trying to make her laugh, but it really wasn't funny. "You joke but...I really am not who you think I am."

He couldn't help it when she said things like that. He threw back his head and laughed. "Sierra, there's no way you can convince me that you aren't the sweet, warm, caring woman I've come to know over the past few weeks."

"I'm not all that sweet," she grumbled, wishing he wouldn't make her sound like a saint. "I'm not really all that kind either." He'd agree with her as well once he heard how cruel her father was before he'd died in prison.

"I doubt that you even had a handful of lovers," he joked. When she blushed and looked away, he stilled. "Is that it? Did you have a lover in the past who..."

"No!" she gasped, pulling away from him.

He still stood before her, motionless. "Sierra," he said with a deep, serious voice, "have you ever had a lover?" he finally asked.

Sierra bit her lip and shook her head, almost ashamed to admit that she was still a virgin.

Drake took a deep breath, taking her hands and placing them flat against his chest. "Is that what you've been trying to tell me?" he asked softly.

Sierra wished it were that simple. As embarrassing as it was to be a virgin at her age, it still wasn't the worst of her crimes. "No. That part might be true, but it isn't the worst of it."

"Might be true? Or it is true?" he teased.

She glared at him. "You've already guessed that it is true so let's not beat that one to death, okay?"

Drake laughed, delighted. He liked the fact that she'd never let anyone touch her the way she'd let him touch her. And he knew that she'd never gone this far with anyone. He now understood all of her tentative touches, all of her hesitation in making their relationship physical. She just didn't understand how good it would be between the two of them. Whatever horrible thing she had lurking in her past, it couldn't be that bad. She was just too smart and sweet.

"It's going to be okay, Sierra," he said and pulled her into a gentle hug. She was stiff for only a moment before she melted into his arms. He wanted badly to question her, to find out more, but he sensed that she wouldn't reveal anything else today. "How about if we ride a bit longer, then I'll take you back to your place?" He pulled back and looked down at her. "Unless you would be willing to let me cook for you tonight?"

She immediately shook her head. "More riding would be great, but you've already fed me lunch. I can manage my own dinner."

He left it at that but the thought occurred to him that he wanted to feed her every night. And every morning. He remembered seeing her coming out of the bathroom earlier today in his shirt and he wanted to be the man who bought all of her clothes for her, gave her everything.

She was too independent to allow that, but it was a primitive reaction that struck him deep and hard. He wanted her, not just for the afternoon or the night. But forever. He wanted this woman in his life and the idea of marriage to her, to be able to wake up with her in his arms for the rest of his life, was powerfully appealing.

"Let's just enjoy the rest of the afternoon and let tonight take care of itself. Okay?"

Sierra thought that was a perfect idea. She felt her shoulders relax, knowing that her secret could be held off for one more day.

They rode through the tall pines, hemlock and fir trees. Sierra knew she should separate herself from Drake, but instead, she laid her head down on his back and wrapped her arms around his waist, savoring the feel of his body. She tried to keep her fingers still, she tried to ignore the heat. But as they rode through the tall evergreens, she couldn't ignore the incredible need to touch him.

"I'm sorry," she whispered, knowing he couldn't hear her above the roar of the engine. But it still felt good to say the words finally, to apologize for what her father did so many years ago. It was almost cathartic as she whispered the apology and she sighed with the release of her guilt.

Drake had to grit his teeth against the need that surged through him with her arms around him like this. He heard her whispered words only because he was extra-sensitive to everything about her, wanting her like this. He loved having her arms around him, even if he knew she wouldn't want him to do anything about it. It showed that she trusted him at least while he was driving her through the forest. That was something, he accepted.

But when they arrived back at his house, she didn't move away from him like she normally would. Like he was expecting her to. Instead, she sat up and he could tell that she was looking around, the sudden silence causing the earth to seem much quieter.

"Are you okay?" he asked softly, not turning his body because she still had her arms wrapped around his waist and he liked them there. He simply turned his head so he could see her out of the corner of his eye.

Sierra nodded her head, still leaning against him. It was as if she were hugging his whole body since her inner thighs were still pressing against his outer thighs, her chest against his back and her arms around his waist.

"I guess I'd better...."

He shifted suddenly and shook his head. "You don't need to do anything, Sierra. Except relax. Come inside and have a glass of wine, I'll start a fire and we can just talk. No pressure. Let's just talk."

She wanted that so desperately, she knew she should say no, should ask that he drive her back to her house and she could put all of her energy into her work. Instead, she heard herself say, "Okay. A glass of wine sounds nice."

He stood up and helped her off of the ATV, then pushed it carefully back in his garage with the other toys he had stored there. She spied a motorcycle and what looked like climbing equipment. The man certainly enjoyed his outdoor sports, she thought.

"I have a great bottle of wine that you'll probably like," he said and took her hand as he led her into the house."

"That would be nice," she said, her eyes relaxed. Nothing was going to happen but they would sit down and get to know each other better. A glass of wine never hurt anyone, she told herself firmly.

He opened the bottle expertly, then flicked a switch and the fire came to life, the flames licking the top of the fireplace. There was even a crackling sound, the look and feel from this gas fireplace to be similar to a wood burning one.

She was just as impressed with this living area as she had been at his city penthouse. "You don't seem like the type to enjoy a gas fireplace but you have a large one here and back at your other place."

He shrugged as he sat down next to her with his own glass, placing the bottle of wine next to them on the coffee table. "I normally prefer a wood fire, but I chose a gas fireplace in both places so I could enjoy it more often. A wood fire doesn't turn off and on as easily so if I only have an hour or two, I can still light up the fire and have a nice evening or afternoon."

She knew that made sense, it just seemed so out of character with him. It was what she would prefer as well, even though she lived in an apartment. "So how did you get into construction?" she asked, curling her legs underneath her. She'd already dusted off her jeans so the linen covered sofa wouldn't get messed up.

They talked about how each of them got into their chosen professions and Sierra laughed about some of the foibles he'd run into as a teen in the construction industry.

They laughed and talked for the rest of the afternoon, neither of them sensing the passing of time. Sierra vaguely thought she might be in trouble when he opened the second bottle of wine and started cooking dinner, a delicious chicken dinner with lots of cheese and sun-dried tomatoes which she devoured after a long afternoon in the sunshine.

For dessert, he made a raspberry sauce and poured it over ice cream, making the creamy confection divinely wonderful. So when he leaned over and kissed her softly, she didn't pull back. There wasn't anything to be nervous about and she leaned into the kiss, telling him without words that she liked it.

But not for long. The gentle kiss could only last for a few minutes when the two of them touched. The chemistry was always there, always simmering just under the surface. Just like the gas fireplace that was still crackling away, their need for each other might be turned off, repressed for a while. But at the first spark, it flamed back to life, roaring so that neither of them could control it.

As he leaned closer, she pulled him down over her, pressing herself against him and whimpering when she felt his strong body cover hers. His hands were no longer holding the wine glass, nor was hers. He'd already taken both of their glasses and put them on the coffee table which meant that his hands were free to roam, free to wander over her skin, underneath the flannel shirt and up to cup her breasts. She inhaled sharply at his touch, but she didn't have the strength to push his hands away. A part of her mind told her that she should tell him no, that they couldn't do this. But she was so tired of doing that. And deep down, she didn't want that at all. She wanted him, had wanted him from the first time he'd kissed her.

She'd been afraid of him, of what he could make her feel. And there was still that horrible honesty issue, but none of that surfaced to her mind at this point. The only thing she could think of was touching him and having him touch her everywhere!

When he pulled the flannel shirt off, tossing it over the coffee table, she didn't even look to make sure it didn't topple the wine bottle or glasses. She just wanted equal viewing time and her shaking fingers started on the buttons of his flannel shirt, desperate to see and feel what lay underneath.

But the more he focused on the skin he'd just revealed, the less she was able to concentrate on revealing her own prize. "Let me help you," he growled and tore the shirt off over his head then took her hands, placing them against his heated skin. "That's better."

He inhaled sharply as she ran her fingers over his skin, but she ignored the sound. Until he reciprocated, his forefinger slipping inside the lace of her bra and finding the overly sensitive nipple underneath. She arched against him as she hissed with the intensity of the pleasure that was so powerful, it almost felt like pain but she didn't want him to stop. She was unaware that her nails were digging into his shoulders until he moved away from her nipple. She had to almost pry her fingers away from his skin though.

"Sorry," she whispered.

He shook his head, his eyes hot and bright as his fingers moved to her back, expertly releasing the clasp on her bra and tossing that away. "Don't ever apologize for doing that to me," he groaned, then his head dipped and his mouth took in her nipple, sucking hard and Sierra couldn't believe how good that felt. Her legs moved up, her jeans rubbing against his in her need to get closer to him. He wasn't waiting for that though as his head moved from one breast to the next nipple, laving that one with the same attention.

"Don't stop," she gasped when his mouth moved away.

"I won't," he promised but his mouth didn't return to her breast, moving lower, downward. She couldn't believe how vibrant every part of her skin felt after he kissed her. She had no idea how he'd done it, but her jeans were a thing of the past and his hand was moving along the inside of her thigh.

Briefly, she thought that perhaps she should be a bit more circumspect in her reactions but she couldn't do anything to contain them. When he touched her thigh, her body moved towards his hand. When his fingers moved closer, she was more than ready for him there. And when he touched his goal, she almost exploded as his fingers moved inside of her. She was on fire and didn't know how to extinguish that fire.

"Please, Drake. I don't know what to do," she pleaded with him, her fingers tracing his back, his arms, enjoying the incredible feel of his muscular body covering hers.

"Just relax," he said, his voice deep and husky as he watched her, his finger sliding into her heat. He wanted to bury himself inside of her, but at the same time, he also wanted to watch her face as she came to her first orgasm. He couldn't believe how sexy she looked, laying here in his arms like this.

He couldn't resist moving lower, his mouth tasting her while his fingers continued to weave their magic and with that one added touch, her body exploded around him, making him ache with how erotic she felt but also so turned on he could barely think.

When the tremors finally subsided and he heard her soft, beautiful sigh of happiness, he stood up, then bent down and picked her up, carrying her into the bedroom. He laid her onto the middle of the bed, stripped off his own jeans and then reached into the bedside table for protection. As she watched, he slid the condom over himself. He would have laughed at her fascinated expression if he had any control left. But he didn't and he couldn't and when he finished rolling it down his length, he moved over her, his arms holding him above her while he looked down into her eyes. "Are you sure about this?" he asked.

Sierra felt her heart burst with love for this man who was so sweet and tender and loving. "I'm sure," she said with finality. She wasn't sure what to expect, but she wanted it all, wanted all of this man. She wanted to have him fill her up and make her feel like a woman for the first time.

When she felt his heat probing, she lifted her hips, too eager to wait. She had to close her eyes as he easily slid inside of her, her whole body stretching, trying to accommodate his length. "It's okay, baby," he soothed when he felt her hands tense on his shoulders. With one gentle thrust, he was buried inside of her. He held still, waiting for her to adjust, for the pain to ease.

He couldn't stop but was relieved when he moved only slightly and it didn't cause her pain. When he did it again, she actually smiled. And when he moved almost all the way out of her, hesitating before coming back inside of her heat, her eyes lit up with the feeling and he knew without a doubt that this was the woman he wanted to be with for the rest of his life.

Sierra wanted something more, but wasn't sure how to ask for it. So when he started moving, she closed her eyes and reached out for him, loving the incredible feel of him now that the slight pain was gone. She loved the way he felt, the friction his body caused. But as he moved more, she didn't like it all that much anymore. It caused feelings inside of her to run into the too-crazy-to-control area and she preferred control. "No, stop," she said and tried to get him to stop.

"I can't, baby. Just tell me what you want me to do and I'll make it better," he said and slowed down.

But she shook her head. "Don't go slow!" she almost screamed out. "Now! Faster, please!" she begged, her hips rising up to meet him, her body throbbing around him in a desperate need to find something, she wasn't sure what. "Faster," she cried out. "Drake, please, don't stop!"

He didn't. Nor did he slow down again. It almost killed him, but he increased his pace, pulling her hips up against him, shifting ever so slightly and was rewarded beyond his wildest dreams when she splintered apart once again, her body throbbing, aching and she cried out his name while her fingernails once again dug into his shoulders. He waited until she was truly in the throes of her climax before he let himself go, reveling in the amazing feel of her body. And when he poured out his own orgasm, his mind couldn't stop thinking about how good she felt, how he had never felt anything so incredible in his life.

CHAPTER 7

Sierra slowly opened her eyes, felt the strong, rough arm around her waist and her whole body started trembling once again. Looking out the window, she could see the dark rain clouds, her mind slowly coming into focus. When the reality of what she'd done, of where she was hit her, she gasped and sat up straight. And the sheet fell down to her lap but she scrambled quickly to grab it once again, covering her nakedness.

She glanced behind her, noticed that she'd woken up Drake when she'd sat up so abruptly and bit her lip, not sure how to get out of this awkward situation.

"What's wrong?" he asked, sitting up behind her. His rough chin scraped her already sensitive skin and she couldn't hide the shiver his touch caused. When his mouth nibbled on her back, then up on her neck, she wanted to just turn around and kiss him back.

"I...um...I can't..." she wasn't sure exactly what she was trying to say. Her mind was telling her to run, to get out of his place before he realized who she was and what she represented. But her body was telling her to turn around, to melt into his heat and experience that incredible pleasure his hands had given to her over and over throughout the night.

"You can't get up?" he asked, his hand sliding around her waist. "I agree. I think you should lay back down and let me discover more of those sexy places on your body that make you scream out."

She shivered at his words, remembering how many times he'd kissed her or touched her in one place or another on her body and she would cry out with the frustration of needing him. He was a relentless lover, almost obsessed with ensuring that each experience was better than the last.

"No," she replied sternly, closing her eyes to try and push away the feelings his hands and mouth were creating within her. "I can't," she finally got out.

He stopped and rested his chin on her shoulder. "You're too sore this morning, aren't you?" he asked.

Sierra wished he wasn't so perceptive or so sweet and kind. She could resist angry, irritating or even insensitive. But when he was sweet and gentle, her heart almost melted.

"Yes," she said, using it as an excuse. "I need to go."

He chuckled. "You're going to try and get out of spending time with me, aren't you?" he asked, his hand pulling away. "But you know what?" He didn't wait for an answer. He simply got out of bed himself, then lifted her into his arms. "I'm not going to let you get away from me that easily. I don't know what it is about you, but I'm going to figure out what it is that drives me crazy when you're close to me."

He turned on the shower with one hand, then dove under the warm spray. "And don't even try to deny that you feel the same way about me," he said as he bent down lower, kissing her tenderly. "I can already feel you trembling and you're hands are clinging to me just like I want them to."

She snatched her hands away from him, terrified that she said or did something to jog his memory about her father's cruelty. Couldn't she have last night in her memory as one perfect evening? He'd been so gentle, so wonderful but if he finally figured out who she was, and the way he was talking indicated that he might do that pretty quickly, he would hate her. He would associate her with her father and he'd be furious that she'd duped him.

As he gently shampooed her hair, she let a tear slip out of her eye, hoping he wouldn't see it or if he did, he'd think it was just the water from the shower.

"This might not work though," he said as he ran his hands up her sides. "You'll smell like me and I'm pretty into your soft, feminine scent. It reminds me of something in my past that I haven't been able to place. But I like it."

She wanted so much to lean back against him, to feel him against her back while he massaged her scalp, making her more than a little crazy. But his words gave her the impetus she needed to extricate herself from the situation.

"I have to go," she said, more firmly than she'd anticipated. But she probably needed that herself more than she needed to say it to him. She quickly rinsed out her hair. She washed her body then jumped out of the shower in record time. Usually she preferred to luxuriate in the shower, stand under the warm water and let the heat relax her, give herself a chance to think about the day and figure out how she was going to get everything done that she wanted to accomplish.

Not today, she told herself firmly. She had to get out of here. She was so ashamed, not of what they'd done, but by the fact that she hadn't been honest with Drake. He deserved better.

"Where are you going?" he asked, glancing at the clock, grabbing a towel himself and drying himself off. "It's only seven thirty in the morning. You don't have to work and you're ahead of schedule on the project. So there's no reason you need to go." He stood in front of her, his body language stating that he was determined to keep her here.

She stepped around him, just as determined to get out of here and work through in her mind what she would have to tell him. She'd already betrayed him by sleeping with him last night. She'd made a firm decision that she would be honest with him, that she would tell him on Monday who she was and accept his anger.

Now she'd slept with him, betrayed his trust. He thought she was nice and sweet. But his image of her was an illusion!

He was going to hate her!

"Where are my clothes?" she whispered to herself, searching everywhere for her jeans and her yellow sweater. She'd had them yesterday. She knew she'd been wearing them when she'd arrived because remembered him throwing the flannel shirt over the coffee table.

She looked all around the bed, frantic to be dressed by the time he emerged from the bathroom.

Unfortunately, her luck had run out. He stood there looking like a dream come true with the towel still wrapped around his waist, his amazing shoulders in full view, and those delectable abs that rippled even as he walked across the room to his closet.

"Are you okay?" he asked, starting to walk towards her. But she stepped back, her hand gripping the towel to hold it in place so he stopped where he was. "Sierra, talk to me. You look like you've seen a ghost but I guarantee that I'm the same man who held you in my arms last night."

That caused tears to slip out of her eyes, dropping down from her lashes despite her best efforts to hide her emotions. "I'm sorry," she gasped out, her head dropping in shame.

"Hey," he said and walked quickly towards her. "Sierra, you have nothing to be sorry for. What's going on?"

"Don't touch me," she said and stepped back quickly before he could take her into his arms. She wanted that so badly but she couldn't let him do that. She couldn't accept his warmth and strength this time. She would have to tell him everything now. Today. This morning, she vowed. "Just let me get dressed and I'll explain everything. I promise."

He looked hurt by her rejection and that made her feel even more awful. "It isn't that I don't want you to touch me, Drake," she tried to explain, her eyes begging him to understand even as the tears fell down her cheeks. "It's just that I don't deserve it. I'm not who you think I am."

85

He took a deep breath and ran a hand through his short hair. "Okay, I'm not sure what's going on but I think you're clothes are out in the family room. I'll meet you there in a moment okay? I'll make some coffee and breakfast and we'll talk."

She nodded her head in agreement, hoping he didn't see the blush when she remembered how her clothes had been left in the other room. "Thank you," she whispered as she padded barefoot out of his bedroom. She found her yellow sweater draped over the back of his long sofa and her jeans were on the floor, right next to where he'd...

No, she couldn't think about that now. Get dressed, give him the full truth, deal with his anger, and then move on. It was a simple plan, she thought as she searched for her black, lace underwear, finding them almost shredded.

At least her pink bra was still in one piece. She quickly slipped her jeans on, laying her torn up underwear on the sofa to be discarded later. Turning her back towards his bedroom, she pulled on her bra and slipped her sweater over her head, relieved that she was already dressed by the time he walked out.

His eyes immediately caught sight of the scrap of black lace and he lifted them, his eyes dancing with the memory of how they'd become so damaged last night. "So you have nothing on underneath those jeans?" he asked, his voice deep and husky, his eyes traveling down her body to see if he could notice a difference.

Sierra's hands automatically went to her bottom to try and cover up the space where her underwear should be. She couldn't answer him, but her blush told him everything he needed to know.

Actually, the piece of torn lace answered his question but the look on her face, the embarrassment she couldn't hide, was pretty cute and answered a whole bunch of other questions.

"Come along," he said and led the way into his kitchen. He pressed a button and the fire immediately flamed to life once again, dispelling the gloom due to the overcast skies. "So tell me what's wrong," he said as he pulled down two cups from a cabinet, pouring both of them a cup of fragrant coffee.

She took the cup he placed in front of her, warming her hands with the heat. She took a deep, fortifying sip, ignoring the pain from the hot coffee because she needed the sustenance more than she needed taste buds on her tongue at the moment. Besides, the burning sensation in her mouth gave her something to focus on besides the anger he would feel very soon.

He busied himself getting out eggs and milk then whisking them together, waiting patiently while she gathered her thoughts. "It can't be all that bad, Sierra. I think I know you well enough to be a good judge of character and you're not a horrible person."

She bowed her head slightly, staring into her black coffee. "My father is," she choked out, another tear escaping and running down her cheek.

She felt his stillness more than saw anything. "Excuse me?" he encouraged. "If you're mad at your father, I can deal with that. In-laws are all part of the package, I know that."

Her head reared up at his comment. "In-laws!" Her mouth fell open and she shook her head. "I don't have any in-laws!"

He smiled slightly and started chopping up onions for an omelet. "You will once we're married."

She pushed away from the counter, pacing back and forth. "You won't," she finally said. "My mother died when I was a child and my father..." she hesitated, her eyes searching out his so she could be clear and not have to repeat this, "my father died in prison."

One of his dark eyebrows went up in surprise. "Okay, so your father went to prison. It doesn't mean that you're a bad person."

"You don't really know my father," she laughed derisively, thinking of all the horrible things her father had been convicted of plus all the other brutal actions the authorities couldn't find evidence of. "He was bad. Really bad. And you don't actually know who I am."

He sighed and put the knife down, coming around to the other side of the counter to take her hands in his. He pulled her over to the low sofa, sitting down next to her. "Sierra, whatever your father did in the past, it doesn't affect how I feel about you. And it doesn't make you a criminal by association."

She choked and shook her head. "You don't understand."

He took a deep breath, trying to maintain his patience but he wanted to yell at her that he knew that she wasn't a bad person. "Possibly because you aren't explaining it to me very well. Perhaps if you could start from the beginning, I might have a better grasp on what you're trying to tell me." It occurred to him that he was having a slightly ridiculous conversation. He was trying to convince a woman he'd just made love to that she wasn't horrible?

Yes, the day definitely could have started out better if he'd had any say it.

She took a deep breath, closed her eyes and nodded. He was right. She wasn't making any sense and was just jumbling this up even more by her bits and starts regarding the real problem.

"I knew you before you came to Denver," she said softly, staring down at her fingers which were clasped tightly in her lap. "I saw you one day at a party my father was throwing. In Chicago." She didn't wait for his reaction. Standing up, she started pacing the kitchen area once again, needing to move because of the nervous energy that was building up. "You must have done something to offend my father, because the next thing I knew, you were being thrown into the back of a car, then dumped into an alley." Every muscle in her body tensed with fear. "My father's name is Joe Berutelli. I'm his daughter. I changed my name when I left his house, not wanting to have anything to do with him."

"No!" he almost growled, standing up and coming up behind her. "You're Sierra Berutelli?" He still wasn't angry with her, but he could tell that his reaction didn't convey that message to this sweet, terrified woman.

She couldn't speak, so she simply nodded her head in shame.

Drake couldn't believe what he was hearing. And then it struck him. The scent! It was the honeysuckle. He bent forward, inhaling her fresh scent but she smelled like his own soap. But he thought back to the other times he'd held her in his arms, that familiar scent that he'd never been able to place.

"You're the girl!" he said with a strange tone. His hands grabbed her upper arms, spinning her around. He'd finally found her! After years of searching and dead ends, she was here in his arms! "How did you know I was dumped into an alley?" he demanded.

The tears were constant now and she blinked to try and focus on him. "Because I followed my father's goons. I saw them dump you off and drive away." She was extremely confused now. Why wasn't he angry with her? Why wasn't he furious? And what was that exclamation about some girl? She couldn't help the jealousy that bit into her at the mention of some other woman.

"What did you do?" he demanded, holding her arms even though she was trying to pull free of him. There was no way he was letting her go now! Not now that he'd finally found her! This whole situation was more perfect than he could have imagined! She was Sierra!

She shrugged, trying to loosen his grip but he wouldn't release her. "I called an ambulance."

"And went with me to the hospital, didn't you?"

"Yes." She wasn't sure what he was getting at, but he deserved to know the whole truth. "I didn't know what my father was going to do to you that afternoon. I promise that. I just knew that, after seeing some of his men run into his office where you'd disappeared, something was very wrong and I had to help. I wouldn't even speak to my father after that night. I moved out the following week and I've never seen him since. I only know that he died in prison a little over a year after your beating. I can't even figure out how the authorities finally got to him because no one had ever been able to get close enough to him to find out any evidence on him. He didn't trust anyone, not even my sister or me. Which was probably a good thing, since we would have turned him in as soon as we could."

"And he would have killed you, wouldn't he?"

"Yes," she said, ashamed that her father had so little family loyalty. Or maybe he always knew that his daughters were repulsed by his activities. She never knew because she'd always been so afraid of him, never challenging him until that night she'd come home after this man's beating.

She knew that Drake would be furious now that he knew the truth about her heritage. "I'll go now. I can see my way out." She started for the door, her feet moving as quickly as possible so that she could get out of his way. He hated her now. And he was fully justified in his hatred.

Drake stopped her once again. He grabbed her by the waist and pressed her back against the wall, his eyes boring into hers so he could find the truth. "You were by my side. All through that time I was unconscious, you were there, weren't you? In the hospital, sitting with me, talking with me, crying for me when I didn't make progress every day."

She couldn't lie to him as much as she wanted to. "Yes. The nurses thought I was your sister so I just let them believe that."

"Why?"

"Why what?" She looked up at him, confused by his questions but trying to be as honest as possible. He deserved that and so much more from her family.

He watched her face, his mind about to explode with the impact of what she was telling him. "Why did you stay with me at the hospital? Why did you hold my hand during those first few days? Why did you read to me, sing to me, tell me all those stories?"

"You heard me?" she asked, amazed and slightly embarrassed.

"I felt your hair on my arm while you slept by my side. Your hair tickled my arm several times but I could never see your face. I tried so often to be awake the next time you came to visit, but I only remember your perfume." He shook his head with a slight smile. "Or more accurately, your shampoo. I didn't know what it was at the time, but I just remembered the honeysuckle scent. It was you. All this time, it was you!"

She was completely confused. Why wasn't he yelling at her? Why wasn't he demanding that she get out of his life and informing her of her termination from his newly acquired firm? "What's going on here?" she finally asked cautiously.

He lifted her up and kissed her thoroughly, enjoying the relief of finally finding the woman he'd been searching for, as well as finally understanding Sierra's fears ever since he'd walked into her office that first day. It all made sense now! "My entire security team couldn't find a trace of you. For months, I had them scouring the city and then widening their search for you."

She blinked up at him in surprise, not sure she understood what he was telling her. "You wanted to find me?"

"Of course! You were there for me. The nurses said you saved my life!"

Her hands were gripping his shoulders but she still wasn't sure why he wasn't angry with her. "Only because my father tried to kill you."

"And you saved me. If you hadn't followed me that day, if you hadn't called the paramedics, I would have been dead that day." He laughed, throwing his head back with his relief. "In fact, I even remember your tears falling on my face that afternoon. It was a hot afternoon in Chicago and you cradled my head in your lap, your soft hands brushing my hair away from my head wounds and you constantly told me that I was going to be okay. When I groaned with the pain in my ribs or my legs, I'm not sure where anymore because I was pretty much in pain everywhere, you yelled at me to not give up. You told me in no uncertain terms that you would be very angry with me if I died on you." He shouted out with his laughter. "I remember thinking that I didn't want to incur your wrath so I fought pretty hard to stay alive and conscious until the paramedics arrived. And then you fought with them to ride along with me, holding my hand the whole time they were working on me." He hugged her close. "I know they wouldn't let you despite all your arguments but you were right there at the hospital with me, weren't you? You're the first person I remember when I regained consciousness. Your voice was what got me through those terrible days and nights."

He leaned forward and kissed her through her sobbing. "You saved my life, Sierra. I owe you everything."

"No," she argued, turning her head away. She wasn't even aware that her arms were holding him tightly. She was only aware of the incredible feel of his arms and the painful wrenching caused by his words. She hated the idea of him being in pain, wishing she could take all of it away. "If I could have traded places with you, I would have. I'm so sorry for what my father did. I will understand if you hate me."

Drake squeezed her tightly, her face buried against his neck and he carried her over to the sofa, sitting down with her in his lap. She was shaking with the force of her tears now and he wished he could help her, to understand why she was so upset. "Hey, honey, I'm okay. Thanks to you, I survived."

"Not thanks to me. My father was a bastard who did that to you. He had no conscience. He was a horrible, mean, terrible, evil-to-the-core man and I was always ashamed to be related to him."

"And you think I should blame you for the crimes he committed?"

"Yes!" she was getting angry now herself. She was tired of waiting for him to realize that he should hate her. "Why are you holding me like this? You should be pushing me out the door."

He pulled her hips closer. "You're not going anywhere now that I've finally found you." He looked at her curiously. "You paid all my medical bills, didn't you?"

She blushed and looked away. "Well, actually, my father did but he didn't know it. I charged as much as I could to the credit cards he gave me. When he realized what I'd done, he cut me off so I sold all the jewelry he gave me over the years. Anything not needed to cover your medical expenses, I donated to the local food pantry."

He raised an eyebrow at that. "I'm guessing there's a story about that?"

She smiled for the first time since waking up. "My father hated any kind of handouts. I believe in helping others. So giving the rest of his money to a food pantry was just my last zinger in his direction." She let her hand fall onto his forearm, her fingers relishing the feel of his skin under her fingers. "So are you angry with me for lying to you all this time?"

He laughed – a loud, exuberant sound that vibrated warmly throughout her whole body. "I'm elated that I've finally found you. And we're going to be married as soon as I can arrange it. We can wait only long enough for your sister to get here."

He said it as if he'd already asked the question and she'd accepted. "We're getting married?" she asked, her eyes wide with amazement at how things were happening so quickly.

Drake looked at her, all serious once again. "I have one thing that I need to tell you before you agree to marry me."

She was suddenly alarmed because of the serious expression in his eyes. "I can't think of why you'd want to marry me after everything I've told you, but go ahead."

Drake held her hands closely. "First of all, I want to marry you because I love you. I've been infatuated with you since I saw you sleeping next to me in the hospital six years ago. But even before I knew who you were, I fell in love with you over the past few weeks because you're one of the sexiest, kindest, most exasperating and amazing women I've ever met."

"Exasperating? How?"

"Point made," he growled before he bent and nipped at the tips of her fingers before folding them closed and clasping them in his larger ones. "But here's the bigger issue. And brace yourself, because you might be angry with me once you hear this." He waited, her body tense as he looked down at her. "I'm the reason your father was finally convicted and sent to prison." He waited as she absorbed that information in silence. "I won't accept responsibility for his death in the prison though. That was from one of the enemies he'd made before he was sent away."

Her relief was intense and overwhelming. A small smile played at the edges of her mouth and she almost laughed at the relief she felt at hearing his words. "How did you do it?" she asked, her amazement growing by leaps and bounds. "How did you get the evidence against him after so many others had tried?"

Drake shrugged. "I wasn't going to let him do to someone else what he put me through. I was in the hospital for a month, then it took me another six months of physical therapy before I was completely back to my old self. And every moment of that time after I left the hospital, I spent trapping your father in his own mess. When I finally delivered all the information to the FBI, there was nothing they needed to do but pick him up. The evidence against him was so strong, and I'd gotten many of his lieutenants as well since I didn't want someone else filling in the vacuum once your father had gone. So I made sure that his organization was taken down."

He waited a long time, wondering if she might be angry with him for destroying her father in such a calculated way.

She looked up at him, her mind slowly absorbing all that he'd just told her. "You risked your life to send my father to prison." She said that with no emotion, her heart hardly even beating.

He wasn't sure what she was thinking, her face a blank mask and her pretty eyes just looking at him. "I don't see it that way." His frustration was increasing. Normally he could read her pretty easily but she was a mystery at the moment.

She pushed at his chest and glared up at him. "You risked your life? You put yourself in danger just to get back at my father? He wasn't worth it! You should have stayed out of it!"

Drake wasn't sure what was going on. "Just to be clear, you're mad at me for putting myself in danger or because I took your father down?"

She threw her hands up in the air in exasperation. "I don't give a damn about my father! He was a low-life criminal who didn't deserve to breathe air with actual human beings! He was a horrible man and I never really had any feelings for him other than fear because of all the things he did to others. But you!" she poked him in the middle of his chest, her fury rising as she thought about everything that might have happened to him... "You should have stayed away! You should have let the FBI and the police do their jobs! You should have never gotten near someone as cruel as that man and put your life in danger again!"

Drake breathed a sigh of relief. She was only angry with him for the danger and not because she actually cared for the man who'd sired her. He wouldn't call Joe Berutelli a father because he'd done nothing more than provide fifty percent of her DNA. No, by some miracle, this woman had escaped from the criminal world and came out beautiful and wonderful.

And she was all his. "So you're marrying me, right?" he asked, changing the subject so they could get back to something more interesting. Like getting her back into his bed now that all the confessions were finished!

Sierra paced in front of one of his windows, her hand pushing her hair back in frustration. Suddenly, she stopped and glared at him. "Will you ever put yourself in that kind of danger again?"

Drake knew exactly the right answer. "Of course not. I'll be too busy making babies with you," he said and grabbed her around the waist, kissing her at the base of her neck, exactly where he knew she liked it. "And you will be too busy loving me for anything else."

"You think so?" she asked, but all of her willpower was draining away with his hands and his mouth doing those incredible things to her, making her knees weak so she had to lean against him.

"I know this to be the case," he replied, his hands moving underneath the yellow sweater. "Despite the fact that you don't have any underwear on, a fact of which I have been fully aware of during this entire conversation, mind you, but I have to let you know that you are wearing entirely too many clothes. A point I've tried to make ever since you woke us up at that crazy hour."

She laughed and tried to wiggle out of his arms. "I'm not done being mad at you. And you should be mad at me."

He shook his head. "I refuse to blame you for the crimes of another human being. Let them take responsibility for themselves. I, for one, am taking full responsibility for buying you the most beautiful wedding dress you can imagine."

Sierra stopped with his words, love for this man washing over her in a wave. "I could go for that," she said softly. And then laughed with delight when he growled, picked her up and threw her over his shoulder before carrying her into his bedroom. She laughed again when he tore off his clothes but all of the laughter died when he dispensed with her remaining clothes.

When he came down over her, both of them naked and writhing together he said, "I love you."

She smiled gently, loving this enormous man who could make her blood simmer with just a look and replied, "I love you too." With her fingers, she pulled his head down to hers and kissed him, reassuring him with her actions that she loved him with all of her heart.

Epilogue

Sierra slowly opened her eyes and looked up at the ceiling, not sure if she wanted to smile or cry.

"I'll take care of them," Drake said, pushing himself out of bed. He wore pajama bottoms now because of just this type of thing.

"I'll help you."

"No, you were up until one o'clock this morning with Mitchell. Let me put them back to sleep."

Sierra sank back into the pillows, grateful for the reprieve. She loved her twins but they were definitely a handful. At six months old, they were both sleeping through the night mostly. But every once in a while, Mitchell would need an extra feeding. Lindsey didn't want to miss out on anything so she woke up as well, commiserating with her twin brother's hunger.

The crying stopped and Sierra listened, waiting. Sure enough, a few minutes later, she heard his deep, vibrant voice. She wondered how such a macho, muscular man could sing so gently to their twin babies.

Unable to stay away, she pushed the sheets off of her and padded barefoot to the doorway of the nursery. She didn't interrupt the three of them, just leaned her head against the doorway, watching and listening as Drake sang their twins back to sleep.

"You're lurking," he said softly when both babies were asleep in his arms, his strong arms cradling one in each arm as he rocked gently back and forth.

"You're spoiling them," she came back, walking into the nursery. "I love you," she said, putting a hand on the top of each of her children while she bent low and kissed her husband. "They do too."

"And you're the sexiest mother I've ever seen," he growled.

Sierra laughed when she realized where his eyes were looking but she didn't mind that he was looking down her night shirt. "At least you still want me after these two," she smiled.

His eyes heated with her words. "If you'll help me put these two back in their cribs, I'll show you exactly how much I want you," he came back.

Sierra's smile was slow and wide, her body already heating with anticipation. "My sister is coming for a visit tomorrow. I don't want to be too tired."

He shook his head and stood up. "Your sister is six month's pregnant with your niece. Take a nap with her later."

Sierra didn't need to be told twice. She took Mitchell out of Drake's arms, cuddling him and kissing him gently as she laid him back in his crib while Drake carried Lyndsey to the other crib only two feet away. When they were once more alone, Sierra turned to find Drake just looking down at his children. "Thank you," he said and Sierra felt it deeply. It wasn't just for their children or marrying him. It was for everything they'd shared since the moment they'd seen each other across the pool from her father's house so many years ago.

"Thank you," she came back and squeezed him, letting him know how much she loved him.

Excerpt from *The Billionaire's Pregnant Lover*

"Who the hell are you?"

Sydney jumped and spun around at the harsh, deep voice behind her. The tall, huge man behind her was more than terrifying. He was....well, she couldn't quite put an adjective to the feelings that were running through her at the moment, but it caused her knees to tremble and her heart rate to spin out of control. She was eternally grateful that she was sitting down instead of standing, although that did put her at a height disadvantage.

"I'm....uh..." She was so flustered, she wasn't exactly sure how to explain her presence. It seemed that the man's sudden appearance and his glaring, angry countenance had rendered her sense to be absent at the moment.

Dominic Carson rolled his eyes, ignoring the lovely woman's pale cheeks and the fascinating sparkle in those green eyes. He was here to work and not gawk at some pretty face that decided to plunk down in his assistant's chair. "Okay, so you're confused. Get out of this area or I'll call security."

He stood there glaring at her and Sydney had a hard time maintaining her grip on the files that she was holding. Placing them onto the desk beside her, she smoothed down her skirt and jerked her suit jacket over the front of her, hoping it didn't look as messy as she felt. "Actually, I'm your temporary assistant today," she explained, clearing her throat when it sounded too mousy. This man didn't look like he would respect mousy.

As she surveyed his tall, immaculately dressed and overly muscular frame, she suspected that this man didn't respect many people, mousy or not. That irritated her and she stood up straighter, unaware that her chin was jutting out with the defiance of his authority.

"You're too young and inexperienced to handle this job. Go back to personnel and tell them to send me someone more experienced." He started to walk away, determined to dismiss the woman. If he'd seen this woman in a bar or a restaurant, he'd definitely approach her. But she was the soft, lush kind of woman that he wanted in his bed, not in his office.

She stood there shaking, offended by his attitude by trying valiantly to be brave in the face of his withering glare. "I was originally assigned to someone down on the tenth floor today, but too many people are out sick with the flu. So when I arrived, your HR department ordered me to come up here and fill in for your assistant. Apparently, no one else is available to assist you today, experienced or otherwise. But since you seem fully capable of handling everything yourself, I'll just take my leave. I'll stop by your HR department on my way out and let them know that you don't require any assistance today, and probably for the next several days since the flu isn't a one day condition."

She turned on her barely presentable, obviously cheap shoe and pulled her worn out purse out of the drawer she'd stuck it into an hour ago. Sydney didn't bother to even look at the man as she walked towards the exit.

"Stop right there," she heard him command.

She stopped, but there was a long moment while she silently debated the issue. Her expanding student loans were the decision maker. And the fact that she had only peanut butter and bread until she was paid next week since she'd just emptied out her bank account to pay her final semester's tuition.

Being a grad student was expensive but this job paid extremely well. It would have taken her through the next month if she was careful.

When he was standing over her once again, the trembling actually increased. She wanted to slap him, to say something that would bring him down a peg or two, but she could barely speak with him towering over her like this.

Dominic looked down at her, noting her trembling but respecting the fact that she was confident enough to stand up to him. He wasn't going to relent though. If she was an idiot, he'd kick her out of here without pause. "Can you type?"

Sydney blinked, surprised by the abrupt question. "Yes."

"And answer phones?" he snapped.

She tried very hard not to roll her eyes. "Yes."

Another long moment of silence where she stood trembling, wishing she could just slap his face and tell him exactly where he could shove this job.

"Don't mess up my schedule," he snapped, then turned around and headed into his office. "Judy has probably e-mailed a list of instructions and outstanding tasks to complete. Make sure you get as many of them finished as possible in the next hour."

Sydney resisted the urge to throw her purse at his back, relishing the idea of how surprised he'd be at the assault. Of course, he'd probably have her arrested, but as he disappeared behind the double doors at the other end of the room, she wondered if it might be worth it.

Remember her loans, she told herself and took a deep, calming breath. This job paid three times the salary hourly rate as the other jobs she'd been doing lately. When they'd offered her the role, she hadn't understood why they would pay so much. Now she grasped the problem. It wasn't the work. In fact, she'd already finished all the items on Judy's list and was working on filing the contracts that had been left on the corner of the regular assistant's desk. The only reason this job paid so much more than normal was because of that man and his horrible attitude!

Storing her beaten up, faux-leather purse back in the drawer, she almost fell into her chair but quickly pulled herself forward. For a long moment, she just sat there, trying to calm herself, get her anger under control. She really disliked that man. She couldn't ever remember disliking someone as intensely as she felt towards him.

She glanced at his nameplate. Dominic Carson. As a grad student working towards her degree in psychology, she'd read studies about both his work style and the meteoric growth of his company. He was a case study in work relationships, which was pretty ironic when she thought about her first confrontation of the morning.

"I can do this," she whispered to herself and turned to face the computer.

Dominic glared at the files neatly typed up on his desk with growing irritation. How had the woman accomplished all of this already? Even Judy wasn't this good.

As he flipped through the files, his eyes speed reading the words, he didn't even find a damn error. How was he supposed to get rid of her when she didn't make any errors!

He couldn't believe how quickly his body had reacted to her lush, feminine form as soon as he'd stepped off of the elevators a few moments ago. He'd never reacted that strongly to any female but her figure, encased in possibly the worst and cheapest suit he'd ever seen in his life, was round in all the right places. Full and lush and his hands actually ached to explore her curves. She wasn't fat, but nor could she be considered skinny either. She was just...perfect.

Mentally, he groaned and admonished himself to get a grip. He had a busy day today with the final negotiations for a multi-billion dollar acquisition. He couldn't be distracted. Unfortunately, even her facial features had struck him deeply. He'd wanted to touch her, reach out and feel her soft, peach like skin. When she'd glared at him with those blue eyes, he'd actually wanted to laugh at her courage. Applaud her even!

He'd never met anyone with as much daring in the face of his wrath before and he couldn't help but be impressed.

Damn, he wanted her! Never had he been instantly attracted to any woman before. From the time he'd made his first billion ten years ago, women had been throwing themselves at him. At times it was merely a nuisance and other times his security team actually had to block their advances.

And now he was going to be tortured for who knew how many hours by a woman he could easily spend the rest of the day in bed exploring and finding all her secrets.

His computer pinged indicating that he had a message. And damn if she hadn't done it exactly right the first time. The woman sitting out at Judy's desk must be pretty smart if she'd already figured out the message system. Judy constantly grumbled about its quirks and weaknesses.

He pressed the message, already guessing what it was. Sure enough, his first appointment had arrived and was waiting out in her area.

He took another moment to skim through his other messages. One in particular he needed to read. From his human resources director, he found out that Ms. Sydney Watson was a graduate student at NYU who had excellent qualifications although not as much experience. Due to the flu virus that was knocking out people left and right, there were limited resources from which they could pull people to assist.

Sydney. He tested the name out in his mind and thought that it suited her perfectly. A bit spicy, still elegant despite her atrocious suit. The suit was probably due to her student status though and not just to bad taste or an innate thriftiness.

A graduate student, huh? He liked that about her. Ambitious, smart…probably an overachiever.

The next few days suddenly didn't seem so grim, he thought as he walked out to greet Jim McMahan, his next appointment. Normally, Judy would send his appointments to him but he decided to switch things around a bit while Ms. Sydney Watson was here.

Sydney smiled to the older gentleman as she handed him a cup of coffee. "Is there anything else I can get you while you wait, Mr. McMahan?" she asked, her eyes smiling in reaction to the twinkle in the older man's eyes. He'd arrived a few minutes early to His Highness' meeting time and they'd been chatting while she fixed him a cup of coffee. He was a very jovial sort of gentleman who was telling her stories about his grandchildren's latest exploits.

"Jim," the deep voice snapped behind her and Sydney stood up quickly, trying to hide the spark of anger that instantly flared up inside of her. Why was he even out here? Judy's instructions were very clear. Mr. Carson would respond to the appointment message when he was ready for his visitors to come into his office. Nowhere in the instructions did Judy say that Mr. Grouchy Bear would come out and greet his guests. He was supposed to be in his cave, figuring out who was going to be shredded next with his claws.

The two men disappeared into the inner office and Sydney breathed a sigh of relief now that she was once again away from His Highness. She pulled out Judy's instructions and read through them once again. She would not make a mistake this week! She would not give His Highness any reason to get rid of her. But if she discovered that he was just too obnoxious, she wouldn't hesitate to simply walk out of here. He needed cause to get rid of her. She just needed to call into her temp agency and tell them she wouldn't work for the man any longer. They'd probably understand. Even applaud her!

Sydney worked harder that day and over the next three days than she ever had in her life! She couldn't believe how much the man worked. And even when he wasn't working, he went to social events, making contacts and sending her instructions through e-mail, while he was socializing! He made business deals at midnight and expected the issues to be summarized and typed up by the time he walked into the office at seven o'clock the next morning.

Sydney wanted badly to tell him to stuff his job, but she also couldn't deny the excitement she felt as she worked throughout the day, trying desperately hard to keep up with the man. He didn't make any more snide comments, but when she wasn't as fast as he wanted her to be, she definitely knew it. There was just something in his eyes when she responded to him that told her everything she needed to know.

By early Friday afternoon, she was exhausted, but still thrilled that she'd been able to keep up with the man. She wasn't positive, but Sydney didn't think she'd made any horrible mistakes. At least nothing he could taunt her with. In that, she considered the week a huge success. Just a few more hours, she told herself, and she'd be free of this evil, insensitive, annoying and arrogant jerk.

"Come with me, Ms. Carson," he snapped, walking by her desk just as she was about to pull out her peanut butter sandwich. She was starving and wanted nothing more than to ignore his summons. But she folded the wax paper back over her sandwich and followed him, carrying her notebook and pen because he shot orders at her so quickly she couldn't remember all of his instructions unless she was writing them down.

In the elevator, she looked up at him, not sure what was going on. "What is next on the agenda?" she asked. She suspected that she should probably tack on a 'sir' after that question, to show her respect, but she just couldn't do it. This man didn't deserve her respect since he didn't give any. "I don't remember any meeting on your calendar." She replied stiffly, keeping to the opposite side of the elevator from him. She hated feeling so short next to him so if she stood farther away, it didn't feel like he was towering over her so much. Besides, his broad shoulders tended to take up more space that she thought he should be allowed.

He didn't bother to look at her as he responded. "Lunch. If I have to watch you eat another peanut butter sandwich, I might just have to throw it out the window."

He exited the elevator and walked out of the building, just assuming she would follow.

Sydney glared at his back with growing impatience. Who was he to judge her lunch menu? And how dare he simply command her to follow him. Well, to be honest, he didn't command. He just assumed she would follow him.

She debated it long and hard. He was already out of the building when she stepped out of the elevator, ignoring the crowd of people waiting impatiently to get on. She should just turn around and get right back on, eat her sandwich and ignore him.

When he stopped at the curb and turned around to wait for her, she couldn't see, but she could definitely feel him raise that dark, impatient eyebrow in her direction.

With anger spurring her on, she stormed out of the building to confront him. Gracious, she commanded to herself silently. Be gracious and professional.

"Thank you so much for the generous offer," she said, her tone laced with sarcasm since he hadn't offered anything at all. "But I must decline your kind-hearted lunch invitation."

She was just about to turn around when he stopped her. "Get into the car, Ms. Watson." His voice was firm, filled with authority that just further increased her anger.

She was just about to argue with him again when he leaned forward and said, "If you don't get into the car this moment, I guarantee that I will order an entire buffet of food to be delivered to your office and will stand there and watch you eat it. So if you don't want to deal with the enormous amount of food I will have delivered so you don't eat that pathetic sandwich, I suggest you get into the car and order something off of the menu at the very nice restaurant I am taking you to."

Sydney didn't doubt that he would do exactly that. She debated calling his bluff, but she just wasn't sure about him. When her stomach grumbled in hunger, she had to grit her teeth at his raised eyebrows.

Ducking into the back of the limousine, she slid as far away from him as possible, not wanting to catch that spicy, male scent of his, or even risk a possible touch by his arm. The limousine was large, but he was an enormous man with bulging muscles on his shoulders and biceps, not to mention those incredibly long legs of his.

A flash of the man naked whipped through her mind and she blushed at the idea. Thankfully the back of the car was dark so he probably didn't notice her pink cheeks but she pushed the image aside, forcing her mind to go over all the things she still needed to get done today so she could finish at a relatively early hour. It was Friday, after all! This evening, she was looking forward to meeting her friends at the bar down the street from her apartment, to tell them all about her horrible week and all the frustrations that had been heaped upon her by this obnoxious man. A pitcher of beer, some cheap, greasy food, the laughter and commiseration from her friends and this whole week could be put back into perspective.

They drove to the restaurant in silence, Sydney trying very hard to keep her mind from picturing him without the suit on. She had no clue what he was thinking. But that was generally the case. Unless he was showing impatience or irritation, there weren't any emotions on His Highness' face. She thought she might have seen a flash of amusement a time or two over the week in his eyes. But since the man didn't have a sense of humor, she was sure she'd been mistaken.

The restaurant his driver pulled up next to was one of those exclusive places that no one could get into unless they booked a table a year in advance. But His Highness walked in and Sydney almost stomped her foot in disgust when people actually moved out of the way for him. The hostess obviously recognized him, gushing over his presence. There were others waiting for a table already, but the blond, bimbo hostess completely ignored them and led them to one of the best tables. Sydney sat in the chair and smiled graciously at the waiter who pushed her chair in and snapped her napkin out, laying it across her lap. She thought it seemed a bit overdone, but she wasn't a regular patron of these kinds of establishments so she wasn't sure what the protocol was.

"That will be all," Dominic snapped. He couldn't control the sharp stab of jealousy towards the waiter when Sydney smiled her thanks. She was stunningly gorgeous all the time, but her smile softened her features, transforming her face into a gut-wrenching beauty that made all of his possessive instincts jerk to attention.

He also suspected that the waiter was purposely standing behind her in order to get a look down Sydney's polyester blouse. It was poorly made so it didn't lay properly on her shoulders. He was relatively sure that she had no idea that she was offering titillating views of those full, soft-looking breasts to whoever was behind or beside her. He knew simply because he'd been the recipient of those glimpses. And he certainly didn't appreciate the waiter doing what he wanted to do.

Sydney's smile faded when she turned back to the man sitting across from her. She didn't want to look at him so she let her eyes wander around the restaurant. "You didn't need to take me out to lunch. My sandwich was perfectly healthy but this is very nice," she said, noticing with fascination that the mayor of the city was sitting at a table down below them in the main area. There was even a famous actress in one corner. "Everyone here seems to be very well dressed," she said, her hand moving up to self-consciously touch her brown suit that she'd found at a consignment shop last year. It had probably been made over forty years ago, but the material was still good and it fit her. Well, it fit her well enough. And the price had been only ten dollars. That definitely fit her extremely tight budget.

When he didn't respond in any way, she turned back to him, her eyes nervously lifting to see what he was doing.

When she found him staring right back at her, obviously patiently waiting for her to look at him, she felt as if her whole body started to flame up with a reaction she didn't completely understand. Her heart was suddenly racing, her face felt flushed and the muscles in her stomach tightened. She sat up straighter, trying to hide her reaction. This just felt….wrong!

"That's better," he said and leaned forward, taking his own napkin and laying it over his lap. He signaled to the wine steward who appeared by his elbow immediately. "Bring us the 2010 Louis Jadot Montrachet."

He didn't ask and the waiter didn't hesitate. Apparently, His Highness didn't need to request anything. His commands were followed by one and all. She tried to suppress her resentment, but she had trouble getting a sub sandwich at the local market and yet he could order a stupid bottle of wine just by raising his little finger.

"You look irritated. Do you not like white wine?"

She took a deep breath and tried to calm down. "Wine would be lovely, although I might just fall asleep this afternoon. I'll blame it on you because a sandwich doesn't have the same effect." She sat up in her chair, calmly placing her hands on her lap and decided to pretend that all of this elegance was commonplace for her. She had been intimidated by the man all week. She refused to be intimidated by a mere restaurant.

He chuckled, amazed that she would dare to be so impertinent. "I'll accept the consequences of our lunch time fare," he came back. "So you're a graduate student. What are you studying?"

He ignored the waiter when he came back with the wine. He absently took a sip, approving of the vintage immediately. The man came around to her side of the table and poured her a glass of the wine, then left after placing the bottle in a bucket of ice.

"I'm studying psychology," she replied, not even wanting to reveal that much to this man. She didn't want him to know anything about her. Once Judy was back, she prayed she would never run into him again.

Sydney was surprised by how sad that idea made her. Why would she be sad that she'd be free of his tyrannical presence? "What did you study in college?" she asked, switching the focus back to him.

"Business, of course. Haven't you read up about me?"

She shook her head and took a sip of the wine. But instead of giving him a set down for assuming she would be researching him, she was shocked at the explosion of tastes in her mouth. "Wow!" she exclaimed, louder than she had meant to be. She glanced around, relieved that no one had noticed her outburst. "This is incredible wine!" she almost whispered.

Dominic chuckled. "I'm glad there's something about me that you finally approve of."

She ignored his gibe and took another sip, still stunned by the crispness and surprising flavor. "This is really excellent," she said again, putting the glass down so she wouldn't drink it all at once.

"Le Montrechet makes and excellent wine," he replied. "Tell me about your studies."

She wrestled with her temper once again. He hadn't asked. Once again, he simply commanded. She shrugged and tried to avoid answering him. "There isn't much to tell. Psychology isn't really an interesting subject."

"It must have some sort of allure for you to have studied it for so long. What interested you in the discipline initially?"

Sydney was relieved when the waiter arrived, prepared to take their order. She barely heard any of the specials he discussed, but opened her menu one more time. There weren't any prices on the menu options which meant that all of them were extremely expensive. She couldn't even guess at how much a dinner in this restaurant might cost so she selected a salad, assuming it would be the cheapest thing on the menu.

"I'll have the chef's salad," she said when the waiter looked in her direction. The waiter didn't blink an eye but simply turned to Dominic, waiting for his selection.

Dominic's eyebrows drew together with irritation. "She'll start with the zuppa Toscana, then the Sicilian style tuna steaks. I'll have the brood di pesce and the seafood risotto. We'll have the dessert menu when we're finished."

The waiter immediately crossed off her salad choice and wrote down whatever His Highness had ordered for her. She clasped her hands together under the table to keep herself from throwing her napkin at him.

"So I'm not allowed to have a salad?" she inquired with false politeness.

"No." He didn't explain any further. "You were going to tell me why you chose psychology."

She leaned back in the tapestry covered chair and looked across at him. "No. I wasn't."

He was so surprised he had to laugh at her belligerent expression. "Why not?" he asked when his amusement had abated.

"Because you are..." she debated which adjectives to use and toned down her initial choices. "Commanding. And it just creates a stubbornness within me that I have been trying to suppress all week, but since you've taken my lunch break away from me, ridiculed my sandwich, ignored my new choice for lunch, it just irritates me. So no, I'm not going to tell you anything else about myself simply because you ordered me to instead of asking me with kindness and interest."

He smiled throughout her whole tirade, enjoying the sparkle in her fiery blue eyes. Oh how he wanted to kiss her and see if he could shift that anger to passion. He suspected that they could light the sheets on fire between the two of them.

"Fair enough." He leaned forward, his eyes holding hers with an intensity that caused that tightening in her belly once again. And a tightening lower, in a more embarrassing place.

With what she could only describe as a charming smile, he said, "Sydney, I'm fascinated by you and was wondering if you would mind telling me a bit about your study choices. I would be interested to hear why you chose psychology out of all the possible degree choices."

Sydney could not believe he'd just said that to her. She took a huge sip of wine and placed it down on the table. When it didn't have the cooling effect she needed, she picked up her glass of ice water and drank nearly half the glass before setting it down as well. When she looked back up at him, he was still waiting patiently, a look of polite interest on his suddenly handsome features but a fire in his eyes that she didn't completely understand.

"Um…" well when he put it that way, she couldn't really refuse him! Irritating man! "I chose psychology because I'm fascinated by human behaviors. I enjoy trying to find out the underlying reasons why people act in a certain way and try to help them behave in a more positive, life-affirming manner."

Up went his supercilious eyebrows again. "You don't think people should just work through problems, push their feelings aside and get the job done?"

And…he was back! This time though, she couldn't ignore his cynicism. "That kind of a response comes from a very cold, very cynical and unfeeling human being." She didn't tell him that he was that way, just that it was a typical response from someone like that.

He got the message. "Are you implying that I'm cold and unfeeling?" he suggested.

Diplomacy, she admonished herself mentally. She had to be diplomatic about her response. She could not tell him that she thought he was a patronizing, contemptuous jerk. "I'm saying that you have a very harsh way of dealing with the world that might not be appropriate for every person."

That comment segued into other social issues and Sydney refused to give in to his rough opinion about the world and how it should run. They argued back and forth about many problems in the world and she sat up in her chair, eager to take him on. She preferred to think that there were people in the world that were kind and generous. He believed that everyone should fight for whatever they wanted or needed and if someone got hurt in the process, they should just pick themselves up and dust off the dirt before moving forward.

She wasn't aware of the food arriving, but she knew that it was excellent. She didn't notice when he continued to refill her wine glass or even that they'd been arguing back and forth in the restaurant for more than two hours.

She was feeling relaxed and powerful when she glanced at her watch. "No!" she gasped.

"What's wrong?" Dominic demanded, his eyes sharpening on her lovely features.

"You have an important meeting in ten minutes."

"Cancel it," he replied back as if the meeting weren't all that important. In his mind, nothing was more important that figuring out how to get this woman into his bed so he could make love to her for the rest of the afternoon. He was so turned on simply by arguing with her that he didn't care what the meeting was about, as long as he could get her into his bed and explore her body just as he'd been exploring her mind. The more he argued with her, the more fascinating she became in his mind.

"You can't!" she admonished, placing her napkin beside her plate on the table and looking around for the waiter. "The man you're supposed to meet with this afternoon called yesterday and again this morning to make sure that he still had time with you this afternoon. He's been trying to get in to see you for months. You can't push him off again."

Dominic signaled to the waiter who immediately appeared by his elbow but he was amused by her forcefulness. "I can't?"

About Elizabeth Lennox

Elizabeth Lennox wanted to be a romance novelist since the eighth grade. She has published over forty romances using her travels throughout the United States, Europe and the Caribbean as backdrops for her stories.

She lives in Virginia just outside of Washington, D.C. and many of her novels are set in this area.

Books by Elizabeth Lennox:

The Texas Tycoon's Temptation

The Royal Cordova Trilogy
Escaping a Royal Wedding
The Man's Outrageous Demands
Mistress To The Prince

The Attracelli Family Series
Never Dare A Tycoon
Falling For The Boss
Risky Negotiations
Proposal To Love
Love's Not Terrifying
Romantic Acquisition

The Billionaire's Terms: Prison Or Passion
The Sheik's Love Child
The Sheik's Unfinished Business
The Greek Tycoon's Lover
The Sheik's Sensuous Trap
The Greek's Baby Bargain
The Italian's Bedroom Deal
The Billionaire's Gamble
The Tycoon's Seduction Plan
The Sheik's Rebellious Mistress
The Sheik's Missing Bride
Blackmailed By The Billionaire
The Billionaire's Runaway Bride
The Billionaire's Elusive Lover
The Intimate, Intricate Rescue

The Sisterhood Trilogy
The Sheik's Virgin Lover
The Billionaire's Impulsive Lover
The Russian's Tender Lover
The Billionaire's Gentle Rescue

The Tycoon's Toddler Surprise
The Tycoon's Tender Triumph
The Sheik's Mysterious Mistress
The Duke's Willful Wife
The Sheik's Secret Twins
The Tycoon's Marriage Exchange
The Russian's Furious Fiancee
The Tycoon's Misunderstood Bride

Love By Accident Series
The Sheik's Pregnant Lover
The Sheik's Furious Bride
The Duke's Runaway Princess

The Russian's Pregnant Mistress

The Lovers Exchange Series
The Earl's Outrageous Lover
The Tycoon's Resistant Lover

The Sheik's Reluctant Lover
The Spanish Tycoon's Temptress

The Berutelli Escape Series
Resisting The Tycoon's Seduction
The Billionaire's Secretive Enchantress

The Billionaire's Pregnant Lover (Available June 2013)